Making It PERSONAL

THE *Personal* SERIES

K.C. WELLS

An interview for Will's dream job – and the guy hiring is his hot client from the night before.

And then things get really complicated.

Will Parkinson has had a tough life so far, but he's back on his feet, working as an escort to pay off his student loans. It does have its advantages, such as the really hot guy who hired him last night. Yeah, Blake rocked his world – several times.

But when he arrives to be interviewed for his dream job as PA in a publishing company,

the guy who's hiring is..... Blake. And judging by Blake's expression, this is *not* a good thing.

Blake Davis is in the closet, and he's going to stay that way. Because if his father finds out he's gay, Blake could lose everything he's worked so hard to achieve during the last six years as CEO of Trinity Publishing. So he'll put up with his father trying to set him up with yet another empty-headed, social-climbing girlfriend. He'll keep using an escort agency when he wants a night of hot sex with a cute guy.

And then the latest cute guy turns up for an interview.

He knows it's madness to hire Will as his PA, but Will really is the best person for the job.

If Blake thought his life was complicated before, it's about to reach a whole new level.

Making it Personal contains office encounters that send the thermostat sky high, a late-night call that melts the phone line, and two men finally realizing what they've found – a love that could last forever.

Making It Personal
Copyright © 2013 by K.C. Wells
Editor: S.A. Laybourn
Cover Art by Meredith Russell

CHAPTER ONE

Blake Davis unlocked the main glass door which led into the reception of Trinity Publishing. As usual, he was the first to arrive, although he knew that Ed Fellows wouldn't be too far behind him: his second-in-command would need his customary caffeine jolt to kick-start his day. He went into the small but well-equipped kitchen serving his floor and mechanically set up the two coffee pots that would be required by his staff. Another grin: how many CEOs did *this* every morning?

With the machines gurgling and the wonderful aroma starting to filter through the kitchen, Blake went to his office. The empty office next door reminded Blake of his lack of a PA, which he hoped to have resolved within the next day. He entered his private washroom and hung his overcoat on a hanger, pausing in front of the mirror.

Will today be the day?

No sooner had that thought crossed Blake's mind, another was hot on its heels.

Just give it up, for God's sake. You know *he'll never do it. He'd have to be at death's door first.*

Blake Davis stared resignedly at his reflection in the floor length mirror, his fingers automatically manipulating the dark blue silk tie until it was perfect. He stepped back, casting a critical eye at the overall effect, trying to ignore the thought that had filtered through his brain with annoying regularity during the past two years.

His navy pinstripe suit fit his contours perfectly, the pale blue of his shirt a good colour against the pearly skin at the base of his throat. The figure in the mirror was lean, slim-hipped, narrow at the waist, flaring nicely to a broad chest. Short, black hair framed a clear, creamy complexion, which brought out the startling Mediterranean blue of Blake's eyes, so blue in fact people often thought mistakenly that he wore contacts.

One last look in the mirror. Funny: he didn't feel any older. Those azure eyes stared back at him and Blake smiled tiredly.

"Happy 30th Birthday," he whispered to his reflection. His ritual thought prodded him once more, prompting a brief swell of hope within his chest, but cynicism won out.

Not a fucking chance.

He puffed out a sigh of sheer exasperation and exited the bathroom. Tossing his morning newspaper onto the sofa by the window, Blake gazed down at London. It was only 7.30a.m., but already the streets below were steadily filling as people went about the business of getting to work in the cold, still October morning. He leaned on the glass, his eyes unseeing for a moment, his thoughts on his own situation.

"Christ, being thirty ain't that bad, is it, boss? Thinking of jumpin' already?"

Blake gave a slight start as Ed's words broke through his internal meanderings. He smiled at his office manager who was standing in the doorway, his leather biker's jacket slung over his shoulder.

"Cheeky sod." He gestured with his head towards the kitchen. "Coffee's on."

Ed gave a moan. "'Ave I told ya recently that I love ya, boss?"

Blake laughed. "Just get in that kitchen and pour us both a mug, then get your arse back here. I'll go through the plans for today."

Ed briskly nodded and departed in search of his caffeine fix. Blake shook his head, smiling. He loved the effortless banter that always occurred between him and Ed. There was no formality: Blake might well be the CEO, but he interacted with all his staff in the same easy-going manner. Not that his father approved, of course, but then he'd run the company along much more regimented lines.

Just then, his eyes alighted on the portrait behind his desk, and the smile faded. His father stared out from the canvas, face caught in a warm, caring expression. Blake gazed for a minute or two at Justin

Davis, the public face of Trinity Publishing, the man who everyone knew as the driving force behind the fastest growing publishing company in Europe. Blake's jaw tightened.

"He's gotta let go at some point, Blake."

Ed's tone was warm and understanding. Blake looked across at the earnest man who was watching him anxiously. Blake pressed his lips together.

"Let's get on with it, shall we?"

Ed nodded once, message received and understood. The two men sat on the sofa, as Blake ran through the details of the day, including the itinerary for the team meeting at 9.00a.m. Ed took notes, Blake smiling inwardly as he watched Ed trying to keep up with Blake's fast-paced, efficient delivery.

"When does that new PA of yours start?" Ed asked with a hopeful expression.

"Give me a chance," Blake retorted. "I'm not even interviewing him until tomorrow." He glanced down and tapped the manila folder on his knee with his index finger. "But if he's half as good in the flesh as he is on paper, the interview will be merely a formality."

"Oh, thank God!" exhaled Ed, causing Blake to chuckle. "And I don't mean to be rude or nothin', but *please*, boss, can you try and keep this one?" Blake's eyebrows shot up and Ed laughed. "Oh, come *on*, we've all read the exit evaluations from your numerous PAs."

Blake felt his cheeks heat up. "It wasn't *all* my fault," he declared, stubbornly.

Ed chuckled. "Boss, they all said the same thing: you're a bleedin' tyrant." He grinned at Blake's expression. "Okay, so they didn't actually *say* that," he acknowledged grudgingly, if amused, "but the general consensus was that you expected a hell of a lot from 'em." Ed's tone became sincere. "Maybe you've got the right idea, gettin' yerself a male PA. This one might have more stayin' power."

Blake looked down once more at the folder. God, he hoped so.

"Happy Birthday, boss!"

Blake smiled as the chorus greeted him on entering the conference room, his team already assembled around the polished circular beech table, all eyes on him.

"Thanks, guys." Blake smiled once more, until he caught sight of the remaining empty chair, festooned with balloons, all bearing the number 30. He groaned.

"*What* did I say? You *know* I didn't want this sort of thing." Everyone laughed, Ed most of all.

Rick grinned.

"Aw, come on, boss, you're only thirty once." His eyes gleamed wickedly. "So I take it you won't be out celebrating tonight with the lovely Melissa?"

Blake let out a heartfelt groan. Everyone chuckled. Damn his father. Justin Davis seemed determined to find Blake a girlfriend, and was forever trying to set him up with various socialites who all seemed to come from the same mould; vacuous, empty-headed, obsessed with celebrities, and not a decent conversationalist amongst them. Melissa Richards was the latest, but the most determined. The entire team was aware of the situation and sympathized with Blake wholeheartedly.

What none of them knew, of course, was that Melissa's determination would get her absolutely nowhere. Not unless she turned out to be a guy in drag.

"This one seems more tenacious than the others," commented Lizzie, smirking. Blake levelled a hard stare in her direction, but couldn't quite control twitch of his lips.

"Now listen, you lot," he began, trying to sound stern. "If she drops by today unannounced—and let's face it, based on recent events that's very likely—play nice!"

He stared fixedly at his team, spearing them with his gaze. So much for his hard stares: six pairs of eyes met his, all containing varying degrees of amusement. It was bad enough when his father came by without warning.

As for Melissa, Blake had tried to drop hints, but they had simply sailed over her head.

"Enough chat, people," Blake announced firmly. "Let's get started."

The atmosphere changed instantly, as each member of the team delivered their updates on the latest authors and contracts. October seemed to be a bumper month for submissions, and Blake was going to have his work cut out for him in the weeks that followed. His approach was very much hands-on, and he tried to skim through at least twenty fiction submissions a week, which usually meant several late nights spent on his laptop, picking at a meal. He sighed internally: one of these days he *really* needed to get himself a life.

He looked around the desk at the team of five people, all of whom he'd employed when he'd come into the company at the tender age of twenty-four. His father's team had all born the same distinguishing marks: fifty-plus, no sense of humour, staid, and with no vision. It hadn't taken Blake long to see that drastic changes had to be made.

And they were a damn fine bunch. Blake had hand-picked them all. Each person had their own team and was responsible for the efficiency and success of every person under them.

They dealt with every facet of the business, with absolute authority to run things as they saw fit. No one came bitching or whining to Blake, they just got on with it. Blake glowed with pride. Never mind what his father said—these guys walked the walk.

"Earth to Boss, come in, Boss!"

Blake started, his reverie broken by Rick's amused exclamation. He gave Rick a mock stern glance, but the tousled-haired young man simply grinned at him, and finally Blake had to grin back. "Sorry," he apologized.

Peter smiled and winked at the rest of the team. "'S okay, boss, you have to expect these lapses of concentration—at your age." His eyes gleamed with mischief as the laughter broke out. They all knew Peter was older than the rest of them.

"Right, that's it." Blake stood up abruptly. "Are we all done?" Nods from around the table. "Then off to work, people." He clapped his hands together briskly. Chairs were pushed back and one by one his team filed out of the conference room, until only he and Ed remained. Ed was staring at him, deep in thought. "Something wrong, Ed?"

Ed hesitated for a second, and then shook his head.

Blake arched his brows. "Come on, you clearly have something on your mind."

Ed lowered his gaze to the table for a second or two, and then met Blake's inquisitive look. He took a deep breath, obviously uncomfortable. Blake was immediately intrigued.

"'As... 'as yer Dad given ya any indication as to when he'll finally 'and the reins over to ya?" Blake's eyebrows shot up. Ed smiled nervously. "It's just that... we've all been talkin', Blake, and to be honest... this whole situation is just total crap as far as we're concerned."

Blake sat back in his chair, slowly running his fingers along the polished surface, not meeting Ed's gaze. Finally he looked up.

"Close the door," he said softly. Ed hurriedly complied and then sat down facing Blake, his expression now anxious.

Blake sighed. "What's this about?" he asked quietly but firmly.

Ed groaned. "I *knew* I shouldn't have said anythin'." He exhaled unsteadily. "Blake, since you took over when yer dad had the 'eart attack, you've turned this company around. You've completely changed the way Trinity does business, and the profits speak for themselves. You're a great boss to work for, yer staff thinks the sun shines out of your arse,"—Blake chuckled—"and yet as far as everyone out *there* knows," he said, nodding towards the window, "all that success is down to Justin Davis. They still think he's in charge, they all think he's achieved bleedin' miracles with the company.... " Ed's voice wavered slightly with indignation.

"So you want to know why I'm running the company, but he's getting all the plaudits, is that it?"

Ed nodded. "I'm sorry, Blake, but this *stinks*! You've worked wonders with this company, but everyone thinks you're the CEO."

"I *am* the CEO!" Blake retorted, astonished.

"No, you're not!" Ed exclaimed, cheeks heating up. "Come on, boss, Justin *gave* you the company six years ago. Said he was stepping down, time to give the younger generation a chance, an' all that shit." Blake's mouth dropped open at this unusual outburst from his manager. "But he didn't tell anyone *else* that, did he? Fuck, he even kept his 'eart attack quiet. And he '*asn't* stepped down. He still waltzes in here, checking up on ya, querying every fuckin' move ya make... " Ed inhaled, visibly trying to calm himself. "Blake, why is he doin' this?"

Blake contemplated his hands on the table, his fingers laced together.

"I think at first he was afraid," he said at last. "Afraid of what the public would say if they found out that the company was being run by someone just out of college, the ink barely dry on his business and marketing degree."

"That's what we all thought, too," Ed admitted. "But what's his excuse now? Blake, you're thirty today. Isn't it time he acknowledged your achievements with the company? I mean, how could ya just sit there last year when he won the Enterprise of the Year award? On the back of all *your* 'ard work?"

Blake stared at Ed. "So what should I have done? Gone to the awards ceremony and told the world they'd given it to the wrong man? And what would that have done to Dad? He'd have been humiliated." He shook his head. "No, I have to trust that one day he's going to do the right thing. And yeah, I'd kind of hoped today would be that day."

Ed was looking at him with such an expression of sympathy that Blake was touched. He gave his manager what he hoped was a reassuring smile.

"But until that day arrives, it's business as usual, all right? Which means I have a company to run, and sitting here gassing with you won't achieve that." He got to his feet, walked over to Ed and patted him fondly on the shoulder. "So let's get to work, shall we?"

Ed's eyes met his for a moment. Finally he nodded. "You're the boss."

Blake smiled again, more warmly this time. "That's right, I am." *So come on, Dad.... Have a little faith in me, why don't you?*

"Good morning, son."

Blake groaned inwardly as his father strode into the office, no knock to announce his arrival, as usual. He watched as Justin Davis walked up to the desk and started to leaf through the papers which sat there in neat piles.

"Good morning, Dad. Can I help you with something?" Blake tried his utmost to remain calm, but his father tried his patience. He took the contracts from Justin's hands, noting his father's quick scowl of annoyance. *Christ, the man just doesn't learn.* "I didn't know you were coming here this morning."

Justin wore an expression of surprise. "Of course I'm here—it's your birthday, isn't it?" Blake had to work hard to keep his face straight. Justin Davis had an appalling track record when it came to remembering birthdays and special occasions. Blake knew for a fact that every year it had been his father's secretary who'd bought him a birthday card. And as for birthday presents? Books. Or book vouchers. Every year. It was a good thing Blake was a voracious reader.

"Dad, don't get me wrong, I'm glad to see you," Blake began, a smile pasted on. "But I have a lot of work to do today, and not a lot of time to spend with you."

Justin's scowl was back. "Yes, and why do you still not have a PA? At least then, you'd be able to delegate some of the things you're doing." His scowl deepened. "And I'm pretty sure that *team* of yours could be doing more. What about that ruffian, Ed something, your so-called office manager? Can't you delegate more work to him? Though what you see in him, I'll never know. The man's as rough as a bear's arse." The derisive note in his voice was suddenly too much for Blake to bear, and as for him denigrating Blake's team....

"I'm on it, Dad. I'm interviewing a candidate for the position tomorrow." He picked up the folder which contained all the details and brandished it at his father. "Will Parkinson: excellent qualifications, glowing references, seems ambitious—he looks perfect."

Justin's jaw dropped. "A man? You're interviewing for a *male* PA?"

Christ, I knew I shouldn't have said anything. "Yes, Dad. You got a problem with that?" No sooner had the words left his lips, than Blake knew it was a mistake. Justin Davis bristled, his jaw clenched.

"Far be it from me to tell you how to run things, son..." his father began. Blake stared in frank astonishment. *The man does nothing but tell me.*

"Then don't, Dad." Blake watched as Justin snapped his head up, eyes wide. "I seem to be doing pretty well without your advice, don't I?"

Blake picked up the morning's newspaper and turned to the financial pages. "We made ink again. Profits are up—again. And the new markets are proving to be a success." He threw the paper down onto the desk, a gauntlet of sorts—if his father dared to pick it up.

Justin's lips narrowed. "I can't deny you've turned the company around, Blake." *Well, that was a first.* "And starting up a department for translating books into other languages, well, it's not an avenue I ever explored, certainly, but it seems to be paying off." Justin's eyes locked onto Blake's. "But I can't say I'm happy about this idea of yours of selling these...*male/male* books." His mouth twisted as he spoke, as though the words themselves left a nasty taste in his mouth.

Blake gave his father a patient smile.

"Have you even looked to see just how much business those books are bringing in? Gay fiction is a huge market, Dad... and it's a genre that's growing more popular all the time."

It was clear from Justin's expression, however, that this argument cut no ice, and for a second, Blake's gut twisted.

If his father felt this way about gay fiction.... Blake waited to see if his father would add anything, but Justin kept silent.

Blake walked toward the door and opened it. He turned to his father.

"Thanks for stopping by, Dad, but I really do have a lot on for today." He smiled, hoping that Justin would take up the hint. To his relief, his father gave a brisk nod and made his way to the door. As he passed Blake, Justin's eyes met his.

"Happy Birthday, son." He paused. "Will you be seeing Melissa this evening?"

Blake kept his face straight. "No, Dad, not tonight."

Justin's expression revealed his disappointment. "Oh." He obviously wanted to say more on the subject, but after a glance at Blake's face, seemed to change his mind. Nodding once more, Justin filed past his son and out of the office, Blake watching from the door as his father exited the floor. He let out his pent-up breath in a long push of air.

Closing the office door behind him, Blake sat down behind his desk and leaned back into it. It had been tough growing up without a mother. Blake and his father had muddled on as best they could since her death from lung cancer when Blake was thirteen, but theirs had not been a close relationship. The two men were nothing alike. When Blake first realized he was gay at the age of sixteen, he'd fought against the very idea. He already felt alienated from his father—there was no way he wanted yet another thing to expand the yawning chasm between them.

As to what made him hide his sexuality? Vivid memories of when his uncle Dominic came to visit. Dominic was his mother's brother and not one to hide the fact that he was gay.

All Blake knew was that his father hated Dominic, and that was enough to keep him in his warm, safe closet for the foreseeable future.

Dates with Melissa so far had been briefs forays to clubs and a couple of dinners. Certainly nothing intimate.

Blake was hoping she'd get the message and give up, the same as all the would-be girlfriends his father had organized in the past. So far not one of them had commented on the fact that Blake hadn't made a move to get them into bed. And as long as it stayed that way, Blake was happy.

Blake took out his phone, scrolling through to find Jenny's number. He stared at it for a second, his thoughts conflicted. It had been a while since he'd required Jenny's specialist services, but right now, he needed. *God, how he needed...*

His mind made up, Blake called the number, smiling as he heard Jenny's voice on the other end. Jenny always sounded as though she was smiling.

"Hi, Jenny, Blake Davis here." Blake was happy that he didn't have to hide with Jenny: the woman was discretion personified. Well, in her line of business, she needed to be.

"Blake!" He could hear the note of delight in her voice. They'd progressed from 'Mr. Davis' to 'Blake' over the course of the last two years, and Blake could now chat easily with her. "What can I do for you?"

"*Please* tell me you have someone available for tonight?" Blake couldn't quite keep the desperate tone from his voice. Jenny chuckled in his ear, as he heard the click of her nails on the keyboard.

"Happy Birthday, by the way."

Blake laughed. He shouldn't have been surprised Jenny knew it was his birthday: she obviously prided herself on providing an excellent service for her clients, and knowing little details like birthdays added the personal touch. "Thanks, Jenny." He waited, more clicking audible at the other end of the line. At last he heard her sigh of satisfaction.

"Ooh, you're going to like this one." There was a gleeful note in her voice that sparked Blake's interest. "He's new on my books, been with me about three months. But he seems to be proving very popular." *Christ, had it been* that *long since he's used Jenny?* Blake shook his head in disbelief. "I take it you'll be requiring his more personal services, rather than as an escort?"

Blake snorted. "Come on, Jenny. How long have I been using J's? Do you even have to ask?" He heard her giggle. "What's his name?" he inquired. "And can he be at my place for about eight this evening?" Blake crossed his fingers.

"His name's Alec, and yes, he's available for that time. Usual rate, okay?"

Blake grinned. "Yeah, that sounds fine, Jenny. Thank you. You have my card details, don't you?" Jenny assured him she did, and finished the call. Blake sat back in his chair, his mind suddenly on Alec and the prospect of having him in his bed. His cock twitched. Yeah, it had been far too long....

CHAPTER TWO

Blake took a last look around his apartment, checking that everything looked presentable, before glancing quickly at his watch. Nearly eight. Blake had no idea why he was feeling so jittery: it wasn't as if he hadn't had escorts from J's at the apartment before. Blake had discovered the agency by accident, as he'd overheard a conversation during one of his rare forays into a gay club. He liked J's. Some escorts were purely that—escorts—and accompanied clients to events, no sex involved. But there were also those escorts who provided an altogether more...personal service, for which Blake was profoundly grateful.

The buzzer startled him from his train of thought, and he pressed the button by the front door. "Yes?"

A deep voice came over the intercom. "Alec here, to see Blake."

Blake pressed the release button. "Hi. Come on up. Top floor, opposite the elevator." He opened the front door and listened as the elevator whirred into life, humming quietly. Within a minute the doors slid open...and Blake caught his breath.

Out stepped a man who Blake could only describe as gorgeous. About Blake's height, 5"11, and a similarly slim build, Alec had short, brown hair and eyes the colour of milk chocolate. Blake estimated his age to be somewhere in the mid-twenties. He wore a dark tan leather jacket over a black T-shirt and sinfully tight black jeans, his trainers fashionable. He carried a duffel bag over one shoulder. Those warm brown eyes regarded Blake with frank appreciation.

"Well, hello there." That rich voice played havoc with Blake's cock: he felt it twitch in anticipation. There was definite amusement in Alec's tone. "Can I come in?" The ghost of a grin played about his features.

Blake realized he'd been staring. Flushing, he stepped to one side. "Forgive me: please, come in." He inhaled slightly as Alec walked into the apartment, brushing past him. The man smelt divine, a woodsy aroma that definitely spoke to Blake in no uncertain terms. *Hmmmm...Happy Birthday to me...*

Alec looked around the hallway, clearly waiting to be told where to go. There was a confident air about him that appealed to Blake: the man seemed at ease with himself. In fact, Blake envied him. He'd give anything to have such confidence.

"Come into the lounge." Blake indicated the door with his hand and Alec led the way into the warm room, glancing around him in obvious appreciation.

"This is nice," he murmured. Blake smiled. The only people who visited his inner sanctum were escorts from J's: his father had never been invited in all the four years since he'd first bought the apartment. He watched as Alec's gaze took in the large, comfortable-looking leather sofa, the thick, warm rug in front of it, and the gas fire which looked like the real thing, set into the wall. Blake liked the minimalist appearance of his home: there was little clutter, and the colour scheme was a palette of muted shades, accented by splashes of colour in the form of deep red cushions here and there, and a print above the fire, an abstract sunset in gold, oranges and reds.

He heard his guest let out a small gasp, and turned to see Alec staring at the expanse of wall opposite the fireplace. Blake grinned: he'd wondered when Alec would notice. Yet another reason why his father would never be invited here... Alec's eyes roamed over the four large prints which were hanging there, evenly spaced apart. Black and white, dramatically lit, they depicted the nude male form in what could only be described as provocative poses, although no faces were evident. In one, there was the curve of a man's nude back, where the eye was naturally led down to the firm globes of his arse. In another, a white sheet was pushed low, barely covering what was clearly a very erect dick. In the third, the model was stretching upward, the wide chest and firm abs leading the eye down a treasure trail to the base of his bare cock, giving only a teasing glimpse.

The fourth was Blake's favorite. It was as if the camera had caught the model on the point of orgasm, his back arched up from the bed of white sheets, muscles taut, his hand around his shaft, hiding the shaft from view.

"Wow." Alec spoke softly. He turned to face Blake. "These are magnificent." His gaze moved over Blake's frame and suddenly Alex's eyes widened. "They're of you." He grinned.

Blake stilled. "That's...that's very observant of you, considering how little of me you can actually see. In fact, you're the first visitor here to realize that." Alec returned to his admiration of the prints. "They were taken by a friend of mine, a very good friend, in fact. He's a professional photographer and we were at university together."

Alec was nodding, his gaze never leaving the four prints. "He has an excellent eye." He broke off from his observations to glance at Blake, his expression quizzical. "You must have been very at ease with him to be able to model like that. Were you lovers?"

Blake burst into a peal of laughter, causing Alec to smile. "Hell, no! Dave is as straight as they come." He smiled fondly at the thought of his best friend. "But he was the first person I told when I finally stopped denying I was gay." He felt his smile shift. "Not that I'm really out now."

Alec gave him a sympathetic look. "Really?" Blake nodded. "'Cause I was wondering why in hell someone as gorgeous as you needed to hire guys from J's. Surely you could just walk into any gay club and be *inundated* with offers."

Blake's heart beat a little faster. *He thinks I'm gorgeous.* Part of him had to wonder if it was merely a line. One look at Alec's expression, however, made his breath catch in his throat. There was no denying the sincerity in that look. Blake gave a shy grin. "I don't frequent gay clubs very often. Not that I ever did in the past, to be honest. It's much simpler to do things this way." Alec nodded in understanding. His gaze drifted over to the low coffee table where an ice bucket sat, a bottle of champagne chilling in it, alongside two champagne flutes.

"Ooh, champagne!" Alec grinned. "How nice." His grin proved infectious: Blake couldn't help but return it.

"Today's my birthday," he explained, "and it's one of *those* birthdays."

"Oh, Happy Birthday!" Alex looked down Blake's body slowly, before returning to meet his gaze. "In which case, you'd better consider me your birthday present to yourself." Alec dropped the duffel bag to the floor and turned to face Blake, moving slowly toward him.

Blake gestured toward the sofa. "Do...do you mind if we sit for a while and have a drink?" Alec's eyebrows arched. "It's just...I'd like to talk for a while, get to know you a little better, if that's all right." To his relief, Alec's smile widened.

"Actually, I really like the sound of that." Alec lowered himself onto the sofa, one arm resting over the back seat cushion, the other lying along his thigh. His eyes were on Blake as he sat down. "So, I have a few important questions, if you don't mind." It was Blake's turn to raise his eyebrows, nodding in surprise. "Top, bottom, or versatile?"

Blake reddened. "You don't waste time, do you?" he said, chuckling.

Alec shook his head, his easy grin matching Blake's. "It pays to know these things in advance." He locked eyes with Blake, and Blake shivered under the weight of that stare. "Well?"

Blake considered for a minute before answering. "Versatile."

Alec chuckled. "You don't sound entirely certain."

Blake shrugged. "To be honest, most of the time, it's me doing the fucking. But.... " His words trailed off.

Alec smiled. "But you like getting fucked, don't you? Though I can totally see why lots of men would want to be *your* bottom boy: you have this whole 'I'm-in-charge' air about you."

His eyes gleamed with lust. "Well, I've gotta tell you...I *so* want to fuck you. So if that's gonna be a problem, tell me now." That smile didn't waver for an instant.

Blake found himself growing hot at the thought of Alec fucking him. It had been a while since he'd been fucked, and although his dick was already growing hard at the thought of sliding into Alec's willing body, he could definitely see himself submitting to Alec. And judging by the expression on Alec's face, Alec liked that idea too.

"I take it that's not going to be a problem," Alec said with a smile. "Excellent. So onto my next question. What do you like? Are we talking vanilla—not that I have anything against vanilla, you understand: sometimes a slow, sweet fuck is just perfect—or do you like things a little more...spicy?"

Blake's already half-hard cock chose that moment to sit up and take interest.

"Spicy?" *Oh, God, please... tell me Alec likes it rough....*

Alec reached for his duffel bag, and Blake held his breath as he reached into it, taking out its contents and placing them with care on the coffee table. Before him lay a dildo, thick and veined, a coil of cotton rope—and a set of leather shackles. *Jackpot....* Blake's breathing quickened and Alec's rich chuckle told him this had been duly noted.

"Oh, I'd say spicy was definitely on the cards for tonight." Alec was grinning widely. His gaze flicked to the champagne. "Shall we?"

Blake took a deep breath, trying to quell the excitement which set his pulse racing and leaned over to open the champagne with care. He twisted the bottle until the cork popped free and pouring out two glasses of the bubbling golden liquid. He handed a glass to Alec who sipped the sparkling wine, murmuring appreciatively. Blake took a single sip, letting the flavour burst upon his tongue.

Alec raised his glass. "Happy birthday, Blake." Warm, chocolate-brown eyes gazed at Blake with undisguised lust, and as Blake raised his own glass in acceptance, he shivered at the promise reflected in that gaze, the promise of what was to come. *Happy birthday indeed....* He watched as Alec glanced once more around the room, his gaze coming to rest on the floor-to-ceiling shelves which contained his books and DVD collection.

"You can tell a lot about a man by what he reads and watches," Alec said. "May I?" He gave a brief nod of his head toward the shelves, and Blake gestured with a wave of his hand.

"Be my guest."

Alec unfolded himself sinuously from the sofa and walked across to the shelves, glass in hand. Blake gazed at the rear view this opportunity afforded him. Alec was wide across the shoulders, the T-shirt straining against the muscles. *Obviously a man who takes care of himself....*

His arms were muscled, his waist narrow. Blake gazed at Alec's arse, the jeans moulded tightly around it as though they were a second skin. Blake grinned to himself: this was promising to be a good night.

"Oh.... Oh my." Alec's tone was hushed as he removed a DVD from the shelf, flipping it over to peruse the cover. Blake was dying to know which one his guest had alighted on, but he didn't have to wait long to find out. Alec turned to face him, holding aloft the DVD, with a bound and gagged naked man on the cover, a spreader bar between his legs. Alec was chuckling as he placed the DVD back on the shelf.

"Oh, Blake. You and I are *really* going to have some fun tonight." Alec took a few more sips from his glass and then carefully placed it on the coffee table. He reached across to take Blake's glass from him and repeated the action. A frisson of anticipation danced up and down Blake's spine as Alec moved closer to him, his eyes bright.

"Don't you think it's about time you unwrapped your present?" His voice had a husky quality that did delicious things to Blake's body.

Blake shivered as Alec bent down, his face now inches away. "Do you kiss?" Blake asked softly, his eyes on Alec's lips, his tongue darting out to moisten his own. Blake was gratified to hear Alec's low whimper of approval.

"I love kissing," Alec murmured softly, as his hand reached down to cup Blake's cheek... and at last their mouths met in a soft brushing of lips, Blake's own groan of pleasure sounding so loud in his ears. Alec's eyes widened and he broke the soft kiss. "Oh, you're responsive. I like that." His eyes glittered. "But I think we need to change the pace, don't you?"

Before Blake could react, his mouth was taken in a bruising kiss, Alec plunging his tongue deep, exploring him. Blake reacted eagerly, their mouths meeting in a collision of teeth and tongues as they reached out to grab hold of each other, both men clearly wanting. Alec hauled Blake to his feet and grabbed his head with both hands, deepening the kiss, his low moans leaving Blake in no doubt that Alec was really getting into this. And Blake's cock *definitely* wanted in on this, too. Suddenly Blake was as hard as a rock.

Alec broke off, gasping, to pull Blake toward the fire.

"Want me to fuck you on this nice, thick rug?" He reached down to cup Blake's burgeoning erection which was pressing almost painfully against the zipper of his jeans. He squeezed and rubbed, and Blake groaned loudly, thrusting his groin into Alec's touch, wanting more.

"Fuck, yes," Blake moaned, as Alec rubbed harder. *Christ, it's not possible to be this hard, is it?* When Alec popped the button free on his jeans and slipped his hand inside to wrap around Blake's turgid cock, Blake whimpered, the sound full of urgent need. Alec grabbed the back of his head and pulled him into another fervent kiss, sucking on his tongue as he freed Blake's cock from his jeans.

Blake's legs trembled, almost buckling as Alec dragged him to the floor, and the two men landed on the thick rug on their knees.

Alec freed his cock and balls, only to begin unbuttoning Blake's black shirt, moving his hands restlessly over Blake's chest, plucking at his nipples until Blake cried out, desperate for more.

Jeans were pulled off in swift tugs, Alec's T-shirt sailed into the air, neither man willing to stop until at last both were naked, clothes strewn over the floor. Alec dropped onto his back and pulled Blake astride him to straddle his chest, tugging at his aching dick.

"God, Blake, your dick is a thing of beauty." Alec licked his lips and Blake watched breathlessly, his pulse racing, as a silken thread of pre-come, suspended from his slit and glinting in the firelight, touched Alec's lips. Alec caught it on his tongue and hungrily sucked Blake deep. Blake arched and threw his head back, gasping as Alec twirled his tongue over the head before tightening his lips around the shaft, exerting pressure as he slid Blake deeper. Alec grabbed Blake's hips and held him tight, his head bobbing furiously as he worked Blake's dick.

Blake wanted to take it slower, take time to appreciate Alec's body, but he was dragged along by a relentless tide. Alec hauled Blake until his dick was plunging down into Alec's throat, Blake's hips pumping as he fucked Alec's mouth, Blake supporting himself on locked arms. Alec moaned around his shaft, the vibrations heightening Blake's pleasure as he slid faster and faster, Alec reaching to grab Blake's arse and pull him deeper. When Alec slid a finger down his crack and tapped against his hole, Blake shouted, his hoarse cries reverberating around the room.

Alec pulled free of his length and stretched across the floor for his duffel bag. He plunged his hand inside and searched, until at last he pulled out a bottle of lube and a condom packet.

He clicked off the cap expertly with one hand and dripped lube over his fingers. He tossed aside the bottle and tugged at Blake, encouraging him back into position once more. Blake sank his dick once again into the hot, wet furnace of Alec's mouth and began to face-fuck him in earnest, his cries growing louder as Alex plunged two fingers into his arse.

"Oh *fuck!*" Blake froze, his cock deep inside Alec, as those fingers scissored inside him, the burn a reminder of just how long it had been since he'd had something penetrate his arse. Alec's mouth was heaven as Blake recovered enough to roll his hips, rocking deeper into Alec until Blake's balls were hitting Alec's chin. Alec moaned as he pulled off once again, gasping for breath.

"Ride me." He grabbed the condom packet and thrust it at Blake, who scrambled off him, shifting along until finally Alec's shaft was in his sights. Blake's hole clenched in anticipation as he beheld what looked to be nearly eight inches of thick, uncut cock, its head wide and flared. Hands shaking, fingers almost refusing to cooperate, Blake freed the condom from its foil and rolled it down over Alec's dick. Alec made a grab for the lube bottle and hastily slicked up his cock. His eyes met Blake's. "Climb aboard." His lips were parted, his breath escaping in quick pants, his eyes sparkling.

Blake nudged forward until Alec's cock slid into his crease. He reached back and held it steady around the base as he raised himself up, feeling its blunt heat pressing against his hole.

His eyes locked onto Alec's face as he slowly eased the thick column of flesh into his body.

Down, down, down he sank, inch after glorious inch making him deliciously full, until at last he felt Alec's crisp curls against his arse. Blake's dick pointed straight up, hard and wanting, and he mewled as Alec slid his hand around it, pushing back the foreskin, its tip glistening with pre-come.

Alec groaned. "God, you have a tight arse." He gripped Blake's haunches and lifted him, then pushed up with his hips, punching the air from Blake's lungs as he filled him completely. "Oh yeah..." He held Blake steady and began to thrust up into him repeatedly, rocking up from the rug, moving erratically. Blake cried out as Alec's cock nudged his gland and Alec grinned. "Jackpot." He pulled Blake down onto him and kissed him, his tongue as mobile as his cock, and Blake began to moan. This wasn't going to last much longer.

"Alec... you're going to make me come!"

Alex's eyes widened. "Then come for me. I'm not done with you yet. We're gonna fuck all night." He thrust hard until he was balls-deep and Blake shuddered as his orgasm hit hard, his dick erupting come between their bodies. Alec held him tightly, hips constantly in motion as he fucked Blake through his climax. "God, your arse is fuckin' heaven." Suddenly he froze, mouth and eyes open wide, and Blake could feel Alec's heat, muted slightly by the condom. Alec clutched at his back as they were jolted by aftershocks, both of them trembling.

Blake looked down into warm, milk chocolate eyes. *"Please* tell me you have a quick recovery rate." He was panting. Alec's cock was still buried inside him.

Alec winked, equally breathless. "Never mind *me*, I'm only twenty-five. *You're* the one who hit thirty today. How many times can you go in one night, old guy?"

Blake grinned. "Oh, I think I can keep up with you."

Alec's eyes widened. "Oh, a challenge." He slid his hands down Blake's spine and cupped his arse, squeezing his cheeks firmly. "Bring it on, baby."

Blake moaned softly. It was going to be a long night. If he was lucky.

CHAPTER THREE

Blake rolled onto his back, his body covered in a light sheen of perspiration. Beside him, Alec moved onto his side to face him, head nestled in the pillow.

"Hey, had enough yet?" Alec teased, hand reaching out to stroke Blake's damp chest.

Blake rolled his eyes. "Oh my God—you're insatiable." He caught Alec's hand and laced their fingers together. "Isn't three times enough for one night?"

Alec snorted. "Oh baby, I'm just gettin' warmed up." Blake stared in disbelief until at last Alec's face cracked into a huge shit-eating grin. "Being honest? Christ, I'm fucked." Alec shifted onto his back and let out a tired but happy sigh. "I'm not sure these legs will be able to carry me home, I'm so knackered."

Blake stilled. He'd never had a night like it. He closed his eyes and replayed his night so far. Alec pressed up against the cold expanse of glass that was his floor-to-ceiling window, his hands bound together with rope which Blake held onto as he fucked him, hips pistoning as he pounded Alec to within an inch of his life. Alec crying out constantly. Alec's howl as he came all over the window, his ass a vice around Blake's cock. At least after that they finally made it to his bed, only to have Alec rim him until he was close to screaming. When Alec switched to his dick, Blake came almost instantly. There couldn't be a single drop of come left in either of them.

But in that last sentence, Alec brought an end to the wonderful sexual fantasy he'd brought about. Alec would be leaving—and Blake didn't want to be alone. He wanted to spend his birthday night with a warm body in his arms. And speaking of warm bodies...

Still holding Alec's hand, he rolled onto his side. He gazed down at the gorgeous escort. Alec's eyes were closed, chest bathed in sweat, which gave his skin a pearly quality. Blake looked down at Alec's body.

He was lean, toned, not an inch of fat on him. Alec's thighs were muscled but not overtly so: Blake shivered as he recalled the sensation of having those thighs tight around his waist as he ploughed into Alec with tight thrusts. Alec's cock lay limp against his thigh. Even soft, it was impressive. Hell, the whole *package* was impressive.

"Admiring the view?"

Alec regarded him, eyes dancing with amusement. Blake snapped back into the moment.

"Let's face it, there's plenty to admire." Credit where credit was due, after all.

Alec smiled. "Why, thank you, kind sir. We aim to please." He winked, but then glanced over at the clock beside the bed. "Hell, is that the time?" Blake knew it was approaching midnight. Alec sat up and stretched. "As much as I hate to say it, it's—"

"Then don't say it." Alec's brow creased. "Stay. Stay the night." Blake watched Alec's smile waver, his mouth opening and then closing. Blake plunged ahead. "I'll okay it with Jenny, if that's what's worrying you. You'll be paid for the whole night."

Alec stiffened but then relaxed. "Do you usually ask guys to stay?" Alec spoke softly, his eyes warm in the lamplight. Their fingers were still interlaced.

Blake shook his head. "No, never. It's just…I…I don't want to be alone tonight." His stomach felt tight as he waited for Alec's reply. Alec regarded him, the moment seeming to stretch out interminably.

"Okay," he said at last. Blake couldn't account for the relief that one simple word brought him. And he knew he was grinning like a fucking village idiot, but he didn't care. "Will it be all right if I leave fairly early? I have a big day tomorrow." Blake nodded in agreement. "Well, in that case…." Alec's eyes twinkled. "Can I take a shower?"

Blake chortled. "You are going to *love* my shower."

All of a sudden Alec pulled him into a deep kiss which had him responding instantly. Their tongues battled, hands sliding over slick bodies, until finally Alec broke away, breathing heavily. He met Blake's gaze, eyes twinkling.

"Only if you're in it with me."

The sound of the alarm pierced the silence of his bedroom. Blake fumbled around until his fingers located the snooze button and he gave it a half-asleep thump.

He lay there in the darkness, brain still addled by sleep. Groping across the sheet, he found the mattress cold and empty next to him. Puzzled, he searched for the switch to turn on the lamp. Blinking in the light, Blake stared, eyes heavy with sleep, at the space where Alec had lain only a few hours previously. On the pillow lay a single sheet of paper. Blake sat up, yawning and scrubbing a hand across his face, his fingers rasping loudly across his stubble as he picked up the sheet.

Blake, it's 5.30 and I've got to go.
Thanks for sharing your birthday with me.
Next time you use J's services? I'd be delighted to see you again.
Any time.
Alec.

Blake couldn't help the small pang of regret that filled him. His night had been filled with Alec. As he stumbled into the bathroom and blearily flipped on the shower, he leaned against the cool tiles as the water heated up, his mind playing scenes of the previous night. Alec lathering him with bodywash and then rubbing himself sensually against Blake, the slip and slide of their bodies together an extremely erotic memory. Waking from a doze to find Alec spooned around him, his erection all too apparent. Alec with his hand around Blake's throat as he took him from behind, slowly sliding into him, taking his time, until both men came with low, breathless cries. Blake shivered despite the warmth of the water. *Fuck, the man is good at what he does.*

By the time Blake opened Trinity's main door at seven thirty, he was his usual self, cool and efficient, ready for the day. Methodically he dealt with the emails and sent memos to the team, before sitting back on the sofa to read through Will Parkinson's application one more time. He made notes in the margin, reminders to himself of points he wanted Will to expand upon or clarify during the interview. He gave his watch a quick glance. Will's interview was slotted for ten o'clock. Blake went to his desk and pressed the intercom. "Karen, can you get in here, please?"

Seconds later, Karen Candido appeared, clutching her notepad, and sat in the chair facing his desk, pen poised over paper. Blake sighed inwardly at the sight of the low-cut blouse, heavy make-up and excessive jewellery. Karen was the main receptionist, and the one remaining member of staff dating back to his father's reign. Subtle hints about the office dress code seemed to have made little difference. If only it were just the way she looks, Blake thought. Karen had a reputation as a maneater, as every new male who entered the company found out to his cost. She was about as subtle as a blowtorch.

Blake launched into his requirements without preamble. "I'll be interviewing for the PA position this morning, Karen, so when Will Parkinson arrives, make him a coffee and then let me know. I want him relaxed before I see him." Blake hated interviews and therefore assumed everyone else did. He always did his best to make sure that applicants were put at ease. "Hold all calls during the interview, and send a memo round to the team. I don't want any interruptions."

"Yes, sir." Karen scribbled quickly. "Will that be all?" Blake gave her a brisk nod and she got up and exited the room. Blake heaved a sigh of relief. At least she'd finally given up on batting her eyelashes at him and making not-so-subtle adjustments to her blouse. Any more of that, and he would read her the company line about non fraternization among staff. The fact that such a policy didn't even exist wouldn't slow him down for a second.

He flicked open a folder to read through the list of new contracts which were going out that week. It made for impressive reading. What was more astounding, however, was the success of the relatively new venture of MM books translated into European languages. Lizzie was in charge of the translation department, and Blake had given her a target of releasing four translations per month of their most popular MM titles. Lizzie, always an overachiever, had set about the task with her usual determination and zeal. Blake had to smile: last month, her department released eleven translations, and she was now informing Blake that she was advertising for more translators, proof readers and screeners.

The intercom buzzed. "Mr. Davis, Will Parkinson is here." *Game time.* Blake stood and straightened his desk, and then gave his silk tie a last adjustment before opening the office door to walk along the corridor to Karen's desk. As he rounded the corner, he caught sight of a tall, lean figure, his back to Blake as he studied the framed press articles which adorned the walls.

"Mr Parkinson? Would you like to—"

The man turned and Blake's next words died in his throat. It was Alec.

Oh, you have got *to be kidding me*! Will groaned inwardly at the sight of his hot-as-fuck client from the previous night, standing there open-mouthed, eyes wide. *Well, there goes* this *job. Of all the fucking worst luck....*

Will composed himself. *Better get it over with.* He approached Blake, hand extended. "Mr Davis, thank you for the opportunity but I now find I have to withdraw my application for this position." His hand hung there, waiting for Blake, who stared at it unseeing. *Come on, Blake, get with it.* He watched Blake visibly pull himself together.

But still he didn't take Will's hand. This was getting embarrassing. Will pulled it back hastily. He tightened his hold on his briefcase.

"Mr. Parkinson, would you care to step into my office?" The look in Blake's eyes told Will the man wasn't about to take no for an answer. Add to that his set jaw. Will swallowed. "Karen, hold my calls, please." Blake gestured with his arm in the direction he'd come from. "This way, please." Blake stared at him fixedly and Will had no choice. He wasn't about to embarrass the man. Nodding, he followed Blake along the corridor and into an office. Blake pushed the door shut and then stood there, eyes blazing.

"Did you know last night?" Will's eyes widened. *He thinks....* Will noted Blake's hands which were clenched tightly by his sides. Oh hell, Blake was angry. "Well, did you?"

"Of course not!" Will burst out, cheeks heating up.

"But you knew you were coming here to be interviewed today."

Will thought furiously. "Hang on a minute, I assumed I was being interviewed for the position of PA to Justin Davis. He *does* run the company, doesn't he?" Blake frowned. Will hadn't got a clue what was going on. "All I knew last night was that I was hired by a guy called Blake. No last name, certainly nothing to connect you to Trinity Publishing. And the pack that came with the application form had lots of information about Justin Davis—bio, company history, press releases..." He racked his brains. Had there been any mention of a *Blake* Davis? One look at Blake's face, however, told him the man was calming down.

"Okay, none of this matters, all right?" Will kept his voice even. Inside he was cursing. Damn it, he'd *wanted* this job. "You're obviously not going to interview me for the position, because we both know there's no way in hell you're gonna give it to me, not after last night." He drew in a deep breath. "So I'll just go now, thanks." He turned to leave.

"Wait."

Will halted in surprise at the urgent quality of Blake's voice. He turned back to face him.

"You came here for an interview. Is this how you usually conduct yourself in an interview?"

This time it was Will's jaw that dropped. Blake was kidding, right? Blake's eyes never left his.

"You still want to interview me?" Will asked incredulously. Blake nodded. Despite his initial reaction, the logical part of Will's brain was already considering the situation.

Okay, so Blake wasn't going to hire him. But Blake had to have contacts in the industry. It might pay to keep on his good side. *When one door closes.... C'mon, you can do this.* He drew in a deep breath. "Okay." This still felt like a crazy thing to do, but what the hell, it was turning out to be a crazy day.

Blake gestured toward the chair facing the desk and Will took it, thankful for the chance to sit. His legs shook and his stomach felt as though there was a bowling ball in it. Blake didn't waste time. He sat and launched immediately into his questions, making notes and clearly listening intently to Will's replies. After a couple of questions, Will started to feel calmer and he grew in confidence, despite the fact that Blake didn't pull any punches with his questions. Will had to admire the guy. He obviously knew his stuff, which helped Will to relax and really give his best. When Blake finally put down his pen, Will was shocked to glance at his watch and see that forty minutes had elapsed. It was a pity about the position: from everything Will had learned, it would have been perfect for him, and Blake would have made a great boss.

"Thank you for coming, Will." Blake stood and came around the desk to shake his hand.

"Just so you know?" Will said with a half-smile. "This has to rank as one of the most surreal interviews I've ever had." He chuckled. "I appreciate you carrying on with it, but I think we both know what the outcome is going to be. I'd like to ask you to keep my details on file, in case you hear of anything that might be worth me applying for."

He picked up his briefcase from the floor next to his chair and walked to the door. He paused at the threshold and turned back to face Blake. The man stood there looking downright edible in his elegant suit, that creamy complexion and those fantastic blue eyes still making Will stiffen in his pants, in spite of the situation. "And I would quite understand if you felt awkward about hiring me again from J's. Though as far as I'm concerned, that would be a great pity." Blake's lips parted as if he were about to speak, but Will had had enough. "Goodbye, Mr. Davis." And with that he exited the office. He gave the receptionist a brisk nod as he passed her desk and then hurried out of the building. *Oh well, back to the drawing board....*

Blake expelled his breath shakily as Will left the office. *Now what the hell do I do?* Despite Will being clearly nervous initially, it became evident that the man was perfect for the job. He sank into his chair and leaned on the desk, head in hands. He'd never felt so torn, so utterly compromised. Then it came to him. He needed some impartial advice.

Blake scrolled through his contacts and called Dave Thurston. When the call connected, Dave's jovial voice rang out.

"Blake, nice timing. I've just set things up for the first client, but she's not due for another fifteen minutes. How you doin', mate?" Blake couldn't hold back the low groan that burst from his lips and Dave chuckled. "That bad, huh?"

"Dave, I need your advice."

Dave's tone changed immediately. "Go for it."

Quickly Blake outlined the situation. Dave didn't interrupt once. When he got to the end, there was silence. "Dave?"

"Okay, forgive me for being obtuse, but what exactly is the problem here?"

Blake gaped. "Er, did you miss the part where I said I *fucked* the guy?

"And? Was he at least a good fuck?"

"Dave!" Blake's jaw dropped.

There was that rich chuckle again. "Okay, answer me this. Does he meet your criteria?"

"Yes. The man's perfect."

"Are you attracted to him?"

Blake hesitated before replying. "No." *Then why is your dick getting hard at the mere thought of him*? Blake pulled himself together, pushing aside the memories of Alec—*Will*, he told himself impatiently—in his bed, sated and perspiring, those brown eyes watching him intently.

Dave's tone revealed his scepticism. "Hmm, yeah, right." Before Blake could protest, he continued. "Okay, my opinion, for what it's worth? Hire the man."

Blake goggled. "You're kidding, right?"

"Actually? No." Dave sounded serious. "He sounds exactly what you need. So what if you've fucked? Are you gonna share that information with anyone?"

"Hell, no." There was no way Blake was coming out.

"Well then, as long as he's made aware of this, I say again, hire the man." Another pause. "Is he out?"

That gave Blake pause. "I'd have thought so, considering his profession."

Dave tutted. "Never make unnecessary assumptions, my friend. Might I suggest that before you go any further, you discuss this with Will? He needs to know that if you offer him the position, it comes with various restraints." Then Dave chortled. "Speaking of restraints... did he push your buttons?"

Blake groaned. "Oh Dave, you have *no* idea." Dave and he had no secrets. The man was like the brother he'd never had.

Dave burst out laughing. "Oh wow, Blake. Talk about falling on your feet. Your dream candidate *and* a demon in the sack. Don't let this one get away. Think of the benefits."

Blake struggled to follow Dave's meaning, until suddenly his head was filled with the image of Will in a suit, fucking him over his desk. *Oh my God...*

"You know *exactly* what I'm talking about, don't you?" Blake could hear the glee in Dave's voice.

"I'm not gonna go there," Blake growled. To his relief, Dave seemed to sober up.

"Okay then, I've told you what I think. Call him up, meet him and let him know how the ground lies. Then take it from there."

Blake pushed out his tension in one long exhale. "Thanks, mate. Really."

"No problem. Any time." Blake heard a long buzz in the background. "Oh fuck, she's early. Sorry, mate, I gotta run. Call me soon and we'll have dinner, all right?"

"Yeah, sounds good. Thanks, Dave." The call disconnected.

Blake sat back in his chair and stared at the folder containing Will's details. Dave made a lot of sense. He pulled out Will's personal details and called up his mobile number.

"Will Parkinson here." Will sounded efficient on the phone.

"Mr. Parkinson, this is Blake Davis." He wasn't surprised to be greeted by silence. "Are you okay to talk?"

Will chuckled. "Well, that decision didn't take long, did it? I didn't really expect a call, if I'm being truthful, though it's good of you."

Blake inhaled deeply before continuing. "Will, I'd like to meet up with you, if that's possible."

"To what end?" Blake could hear the sudden tired note in Will's voice. He couldn't blame him.

"Will, I'd like to offer you the job." He heard the hitch in Will's breathing. Before the man could say anything else, Blake plunged ahead. "But before you give me an answer, I feel there are certain conditions we must discuss. If, after that, you're happy to take up the offer, then we'll get you started right away."

"You're not kidding, are you?" Will spoke quietly. There was something in his voice, an almost hopeful quality.

"Not in the slightest," Blake affirmed. "Will you meet me?"

"Yes." No hesitation. "When and where?"

Blake thought quickly. He didn't want to do this at the office.

"Can you come to my apartment tonight, about seven? We can chat and eat, if you like. If you're going to work with me, I want to get to know you."

There was a pause before Will answered. "*Just* dinner and talking?"

"Yes. This is business." Blake waited, suddenly nervous to hear Will's reply.

At last Will replied. "Okay. Seven it is."

Blake let his pent-up breath escape. "Great. I'll see you then." They exchanged a few brief words and he disconnected the call. He put his phone on the desk and stared at it for a moment. Despite Dave's reassuring words, Blake was nervous. He hoped to God he wasn't about to make a huge mistake.

CHAPTER FOUR

Will came through the main door to Blake's building and stopped. Unlike the previous night, there was a doorman on duty, his feet up on the front desk, watching a small TV. His gaze snapped upward at Will's approach.

"Good evening, sir. Can I help you?"

Will gave him a friendly smile. "I'm here to see Blake Davis, top floor."

The doorman nodded. "Mr. Davis told me to expect you, sir. Go right on up." Will dipped his chin in acknowledgment and headed for the elevator. His stomach was in knots for the third time in twenty-four hours. Waiting for his interview that morning had been nerve-racking enough, but that was nothing compared to his state the previous evening. He knew he came across as calm and confident, but it was an act, nothing more. Thankfully Blake had helped dissipate his nerves. Will was floundering in the dark right now, having no clue what was coming at him. *What does he want to discuss*? It had occurred to him when Blake suggested dinner that he wanted to get him in the sack once more, but Will dismissed the thought almost instantaneously. Even on the evidence of such a short acquaintance, Blake appeared to have more integrity than that. Will closed his eyes, taking calming breaths as the elevator made its smooth journey up to the top floor. When the doors slid open, he stepped out and raised his hand to knock, only to pause before his hand made contact with the door. He dragged air into his lungs. *C'mon, get it together.*

The door opened unexpectedly and Blake stood there, dressed in jeans and a blue shirt that matched his eye colour. Will's cock hardened at the sight. *Does the man have to be so fucking beautiful*? It was the only word that did him justice.

Blake smiled. "Right on time. Come on in."

He followed Blake into the lounge where the gas fire was burning, its warmth spilling out into the room. Will sniffed up appreciatively. Something smelled good.

"It's only chicken from the local deli." There was an apologetic note to Blake's voice. "With green beans and sautéed potatoes." Will's stomach growled and his cheeks heated up. Blake chuckled. "Want to eat while we talk?"

"Sounds good." Will was famished. Blake led the way into a small room off the lounge which Will hadn't noticed the previous night. *Hardly surprising, I was too busy fucking.* The thought didn't help cool his burning cheeks for an instant. He stared at the dining table surrounded by four chairs, the table set for two. Wine glasses stood on coasters.

"I wasn't sure if you would be driving tonight. I know we had champagne last night. There's juice or water if you'd prefer."

Will liked Blake's manner. Something about the man put Will at his ease.

"Juice would be great."

Blake smiled once more and disappeared off into what had to be the kitchen. Will sat and spread the white napkin over his lap, just as Blake returned with a glass of juice.

Once it was handed over, he disappeared once more, returning with two plates piled with chicken and vegetables, the aroma of lemon and garlic making Will's mouth water.

They ate slowly, Will relishing every bite. "This is delicious."

Blake finished his current mouthful before speaking. "I usually eat this once a week. It's quick if I have work to do and no time to cook."

"Do you work most evenings?" Will forked another morsel of chicken, savouring the subtle flavours.

Blake nodded. "Unfortunately, right now I have no work-life balance. The job tends to take over everything."

"Then it's a good thing you're taking me on, isn't it?" Will placed his fork against the plate and regarded Blake for a moment. "You *were* serious, weren't you? About the job?"

"Of course!" Blake seemed surprised by the question. "Did you think I was pulling your leg or something?" He stared at Will in silence for a second or two.

Will leaned back into his chair. "To be honest, I was shocked when you rang. It was the last thing I expected to hear." He regarded Blake keenly. "Though I have to say, I'm intrigued to know what you want to discuss."

Blake put down his cutlery and gazed frankly at Will. "You know I'm not out." Will nodded. He remembered him saying as much. "I'd like it to stay that way. If you accept the position, it's on the proviso that no one must learn what happened between us."

Will nodded. "I'm out, but I'm not about to prance into the office, waving a rainbow flag and wearing mascara and nail polish, if that's what you're worried about." A thought struck him. "We would be working closely together. You're afraid that if your staff know I'm gay, they might wonder about you, too. Gay by association, almost."

Blake's eyes lit up. "Yes, exactly." Will heard the relief in his words.

"I don't have a problem with that. But you should know, if someone asks—not that I'm saying they will, it depends how well their gaydar is functioning, because I certainly won't make it obvious—I'm not sure how I would feel about denying it." Will had come to terms with his sexuality a long time—and a whole other lifetime—ago.

Blake regarded him in silence, and Will wondered what was going on in his head. He genuinely liked the man, and he knew in that instance he would do everything in his power to keep his new boss firmly in the closet, if that was what he wanted.

"That's acceptable," Blake said at last, and Will breathed more easily.

Their meal finished, Will went into the lounge while Blake made coffee. They sat on the sofa, sipping the aromatic brew and gazing at the flickering flames.

Will looked down at the rug and his dick hardened at the memory of Blake riding his cock. Christ, had that only been twenty-four hours ago?

He tried to ignore the images in his head, but a quick look at Blake told him much. Blake stared at the rug, his cheeks red, lips parted. Will gave a surreptitious glance at Blake's crotch. The man was plainly hard. Will groaned inwardly. He hadn't even started the job and his boss was already giving him a stiffy.

"Can I ask you something?" Blake's question cut through his internal meanderings. Will twisted to face him, nodding. "Why do you do the escort thing?"

Oh hell. Will swallowed. "I finished university with a pretty hefty debt, thanks to my student loans, and although I had a job with a publishing company, it wasn't even making a dent in it. Someone suggested I try doing escort work." He mentally crossed his fingers, praying for no more questions on the subject. His heart sank when Blake spoke.

"Do you intend to continue with it, once you start working for me?"

Will became still. He didn't want to lie. That was no basis for a working relationship. "If I'm honest, I'll have to say yes, although I can promise you it will *never* compromise my job at Trinity." He met Blake's gaze. "If that's not acceptable, then tell me now and we'll call it a day." He waited anxiously for his response.

Blake looked down at the floor for the longest while, which caused Will's chest to tighten. When Blake finally raised his head to look at him, Will's heart was in his mouth.

"There will be days when we have to work late, you understand. And there will be business trips to book fairs in Europe. So it won't be a regular hours kind of job." Will nodded.

"Well, as long as I have your word that the job will come first, then yes, I can live with that."

Will could have kissed him. "Thank you," he said, shaking with relief.

Blake grinned. "So does that mean you are officially accepting my job offer, Mr. Parkinson?" His eyes gleamed.

Will returned his grin. "Yes, Mr. Davis. It would be a pleasure. When do I start?"

Blake chuckled. "Tomorrow morning. I'm usually there by seven thirty, and Ed Fellows, the office manager, isn't far behind. The rest of the staff are there by eight thirty. That will include you."

Will determined there and then that if Blake started work at seven thirty, so would he. Not that he was about to tell Blake that. He'd surprise him tomorrow morning. He glanced at his watch. "In that case, I might go home and get a good night's sleep. Want to make a good impression on the boss on my first day." He winked.

Will was dying to ask Blake if he would ever hire his services again. The previous night had been a revelation. He'd never expected to find so responsive a client, and it had shaken him to connect so intimately with Blake. Not that Blake would ever know that. Nor would Will ever tell his new boss the full extent of his experience with J's. In fact, if last night was anything to go by, Will wasn't sure he could do that again, despite his experience. Because after one night with Blake, he was hungry for more, and the thought of being with someone else wrenched him hard.

Will was pleased to see Blake's eyebrows shoot up when he caught sight of Will leaning against the glass door of the office when Blake arrived. Better yet was the approving look Blake gave him.

"I'm impressed."

Will shrugged nonchalantly, secretly pleased. Blake unlocked the door and led him into the office. He paused at the door to the kitchen and turned to Will.

"I learned pretty fast that if I have the coffee ready and waiting, this bunch were much more enthusiastic about getting to work on time." He winked. "Especially Ed. The man loves his caffeine."

"You maligning' me again, boss?"

Will turned at the sound of a gruff voice behind him. This was clearly Ed Fellows, Blake's right hand man. Blake had given him the lowdown on all the team the previous night, so that Will wasn't walking in blind. Ed looked like he was probably the same age as Blake, with green eyes and short brown hair. Will noted the dark swirl of a tattoo beneath Ed's shirt. Blake had summed up Ed in three words—loyal, rough, committed—and he obviously trusted Ed implicitly with the smooth day-to-day running of the office. Will held out his hand to greet him and Ed shook it with a tight grip.

"Well, mate, I for one am bleedin' delighted to 'ave you 'ere. Maybe now I can get on with me job and leave you to deal with 'is 'ighness over there."

Will had to smile. Ed's manner was such a refreshing change to the stuffed shirts he'd worked with in his last job. The small publishing company had been a great first step. However, Will had seen where they could have made huge leaps forward in their business, but there'd been so much resistance it had been a daily slog to make even the slightest change. He already liked Ed's way of speaking, and it was clear he and Blake had a great working relationship.

"Pleased to meet you, Ed. I'm Will Parkinson."

Ed grinned. "Just do us all a favour, Will, and stick around. An' don't put up with any shit from the boss. He may crack the whip sometimes but underneath he's about as ruthless as a kitten." Ed winked at Blake who was shaking his head, but even Will could tell he wasn't offended by Ed's words. Ed watched Blake fill up the coffee machine. "Coffee not on yet, boss? You're slippin'." His eyes sparkled.

Blake emitted a low growl. "Any more of your lip and you can make it yourself." The twitch of his lips gave him away, however. The machine started gurgling, the aroma of coffee already in the air. Blake beckoned to Will with a crooked finger. "Come see your office." He gave Ed a brief nod and then led Will out of the kitchen and along the corridor to the office next to his.

Will took a look around. It wasn't huge, but then he didn't need huge. There was an identical window to the one in Blake's office, a wide desk in front of it and two chairs. Two filing cabinets stood against the wall, and beside them a door connecting the two offices. Next to the desk was a workstation with a printer and scanner.

Will smiled. This would do nicely.

"If you want to add some stuff from home to make it seem more like your own space, feel free," Blake suggested. Will was way ahead of him. There was a space on his desk next to the computer monitor that was perfect for his peace lily, and he could put his potted gardenia on top of the filing cabinet. There was plenty of light for it.

Blake opened the connecting door to his office and waved Will through. "We have a team meeting every morning at nine. Not a long, drawn out affair, but a chance for everyone to give updates on progress." He glanced at his watch. "Maybe it would be a good use of our time if we spent a while until then bringing you up to speed with current projects and issues that will require your attention. I can give you a little more detail about the day-to-day running of this place." Will nodded. Blake struck him as extremely well organized and efficient, which suited him fine.

Blake sat at his desk, Will facing him. "So my typical day is spent managing submissions, and that is something I don't delegate." Will nodded in acknowledgment. "I also manage the contracts and the various departments that keep everything else moving. You'll meet the team shortly." He met Will's gaze. "When I came into the company, it was a traditional publishing house, producing fiction hardback and paperback books. My father had resisted introducing e-books: he claimed it would never be that popular. Yeah, right." Both men smirked and then Blake's expression grew more serious. "We're not a huge company, Will."

"Maybe not," Will interjected, "but you're growing. You have close to one thousand employees, authors and contractors, and the list grows daily." Blake's eyes glittered with approval. Will had done his homework. He knew that Trinity was the rising star in the publishing world. That was one of the main reasons he'd applied for the position.

"Exactly. My job is spent making sure all those people keep moving at a pace that produces books as they are scheduled. *Your* job is to keep me on track. You'll need to work closely with the team. If issues arise, *you* will be the first port of call."

"You mentioned book fairs yesterday."

Blake grinned. "Yeah, I hope you like traveling." Will's eyes lit up. It was one aspect of the job that really appealed to him. "Have you ever attended a major trade show?"

"Been to a car show once or twice."

Blake nodded. "Then you'll understand the concept of the book fairs. 100,000 plus people under one roof. You've actually just missed the Frankfurt book fair—that was last week—and there were three times that number attending. Twenty-five thousand vendors. Every aspect of the book business was represented there, from printing to warehousing to management software."

Will nodded. He couldn't wait to attend such an event.

"It's a big deal," Blake continued. "Libraries, bookstores, distributors—they do eighty percent of their yearly purchasing and business contracts during or based on the meetings at the fair."

He ticked items off on his fingers. "We're talking setting up foreign rights contracts, checking out production contracts based on who has the best rates for printing... It's a truly mind-boggling event."

Will grinned. "But you love it."

Blake returned his grin. "Yeah, but it's exhausting. I basically show up on day one with a smile and close my eyes for the first time five days later. The vendor floor runs from nine to five, but then there are dinners. Actually, sometimes it's dinner with one person, dessert with another and drinks with a third. Not to mention that I start the day with a breakfast meeting." His face wore a rueful expression. "I probably eat and drink more during book fairs than I normally would in a month."

Will couldn't resist. "Yeah, but it doesn't show." He waggled his eyebrows and Blake's mouth dropped open. He waved a warning finger at Will, who held up both hands. "Sorry." Blake said nothing, but Will liked that gleam in his boss's eyes.

They spent the next fifty minutes going through Blake's present list of submissions, and Will noted the contracts to be issued, ready for passing on to the team.

The purposeful working atmosphere in the office was pleasant and Will felt at ease almost instantly. He got a good feeling about this job. Of course, the fact that he had the hots for his boss didn't enter into it. It was a struggle to look at Blake and not be reminded of their night together.

Will had no clue how the man had gotten under his skin so fast, but there was no denying it: that night had been the best sex of his life to date. Sex that hot was difficult to walk away from, and Will found himself hoping, more than once, that Blake would be happy to use his services again. The more logical part of his brain held no such illusions. Blake wouldn't want to mix business with pleasure. Damn....

It was time for the team meeting and Will followed Blake into the conference room.

"Grab yourself a coffee before they all get here," Blake advised, but it seemed Ed was ahead of them. He entered the office bearing two mugs which he handed to Blake and Will.

"Thought you might want these before that bunch of hyenas drink the lot," he said with a wink. Will gave him a grateful look and took a long drink of his coffee. He was surprised to find his mouth was suddenly dry, coupled with a fluttery sensation in his stomach. As the team began to file into the room, chatting animatedly, Will took several long breaths in an effort to quell the rising tide of nerves.

"Morning, all." Blake took a seat and gestured for Will to take the empty one to his right. "Before we get started, I'd like to introduce my new PA, Will Parkinson, who is starting with us today. I'm sure you'll make him feel welcome. And just so you know? I dished all the gossip on you guys yesterday so he knows what to expect." He gave an evil grin and everyone laughed. "It might be an idea to go around the table and introduce yourselves, so he can put faces to the names."

"Well, 'e's already met the cream of the crop," said Ed with a wink, buffing his fingernails on his shirt. He was greeted with loud guffaws. "Apart from office manager, I'm head of admin."

Next to him was an auburn-haired woman in her mid-twenties. "Hi, Will, welcome aboard. I'm Lizzie." Her accent was delightful. "As you can no doubt hear, I'm not from around here. I'm Belgian. I'm in charge of foreign rights and translations." Will gave her a polite nod. Each member of the team gave their name and their job title. Peter, a tall man in his early thirties, was in charge of art design. Will liked his no-nonsense manner straight away. Rick was next, all tousled hair and big blue eyes. He gave the impression of being the youngest one and Will had to admit he was definitely cute. Rick was in charge of marketing and promotion. Then came Beth, head of the editing department. She gave Will an easy smile. Finally there was Stephen, in charge of distribution. Stephen seemed very laid back. Will liked that.

"Okay, that's it for all the introductions." Blake took charge once more, his manner brisk. "Let's get on with it." Will listened as each member of the team gave their updates. He jotted down details, making a mental note to meet up with each person during the coming week to get a better feel for their teams. They seemed to be a dedicated group, personable and intelligent. Will was pleased to note his nerves had disappeared altogether.

A knock at the door drew his attention. It was the receptionist, Karen, whom he'd met the day before. Her style of dress hadn't improved.

Will thought the tight blouse and even tighter short skirt not entirely appropriate for her position—or her age, come to think of it. After all, she was the first person to greet any visitors to the building, and as first impressions went, her appearance was at odds with the rest of the staff that Will had met so far. Maybe he'd talk to Blake about it.

"Karen has been doubling up as my secretary until the PA position was filled," Blake was explaining.

"So my job has gotten a lot easier as of today," Karen purred, batting her eyelashes at Will. He gave her a tight smile. To Will's relief, Blake stepped in.

"All calls to me will now to directed through to Will's office. If there are any issues arising throughout the day, please ensure that he's kept informed. And if you require any information as to my schedule, you'll go to Will." Blake was addressing everyone in the room.

Will appreciated Blake's words. The two of them would be working closely together and Blake was making sure everyone knew that if they wanted Blake, they had to go through Will first. His chest swelled. He was overjoyed to have the job and determined not to let Blake down.

And if Blake wanted things to remain purely professional between them, well, Will would have to accept that.

It didn't mean he had to like it, though.

CHAPTER FIVE

Will stifled a groan as Karen appeared yet again in his doorway. This had to be her fourth visit that morning. He kept his expression politely neutral. "Karen, what can I do for you?" He sighed inwardly as she walked slowly up to his desk, hips rolling suggestively. Not for the first time, Will wished he was out at work. At least then he could tell her where the rubber met the road, and get her to stop flirting with him. He'd been there for one day before it had started and nearly two weeks later, it was starting to rile him.

"Sorry to disturb you, Will, but I've had a couple of calls from some of our authors with queries about their release dates." Karen's voice was husky, and Will had to wonder if she thought it made her sound alluring. "I took down their details." She leaned on his desk on her elbows, her ample bosom nearly spilling out of the silky top which barely contained it.

"Thanks, Karen, but you didn't have to leave your desk to come tell me. You could have called me, or emailed the information." Will made sure nothing in his voice or expression could give her the wrong impression, gazing steadfastly at her face. But *my God*, the temptation to shout at her, '*Lady, I'm gay, will you just get those heaving breasts out of my face?*' was overpowering. He held out his hand for the message slips that she'd brought with her. Karen handed them over with a look of extreme reluctance. "Thank you," he said sincerely. "I'll make sure these get to Blake."

She pouted and left the room, giving that substantial arse an extra wiggle as she did so. When he was certain she was no longer in earshot, Will sagged back into his chair with a long, heavy sigh. Thank God Lizzie and Beth were nothing like her. In fact, the whole team was a delight to work with. Will had quickly becoming accustomed to Lizzie's quiet manner, Rick's teasing asides and Ed's loud Cockney ways. And as for his boss... Will felt as though the job had been waiting for him his entire life: he simply slotted into his allotted space and got on with it.

"She *is* a handful, isn't she?"

Peter leaned against the doorjamb, coffee mug in hand, a look of distinct amusement etched across his face. Will finally gave way to the groan which had been demanding to be set free.

"Is she like that with everyone?"

Peter chuckled. "Sorry, Will, but it's par for the course around here. Karen's come on to every bloke at one point or another." He regarded Will over the top of his rimless glasses. "But she seems to be more tenacious with you." That smirk was not helping. "And what makes it worse? I'm pretty sure she has a boyfriend."

Will shuddered. Enough of Karen. "What can I do for you?"

Peter straightened. "Is Blake all right?" His forehead creased.

Will arched his brows. "What do you mean?"

"I caught sight of him coming out of the kitchen and I thought there was something up. It's probably nothing, but... "

Will considered this. He hadn't spoken with Blake for the past hour. Come to think of it, the closed door between their offices wasn't usual.

"I'll take him a coffee and see if I can glean what's up." Peter gave him a grateful look and promptly left him alone. Will got up and went into the kitchen to pour Blake a coffee before walking back into his office and approaching the adjoining door, knocking softly. No answer. Will opened the door and blinked in surprise. The room was darkened, the blinds drawn completely over the windows. Will slipped into the room. Blake wasn't at his desk, but Will soon spied him. Blake was stretched out on the sofa, arm over his eyes.

"Blake?" Will spoke softly, barely above a whisper. Something was definitely wrong.

Blake whimpered, a sound full of pain. Will put down the mug on the desk and moved to the sofa, dropping to his knees beside Blake. "What's wrong?" He kept his voice as quiet as possible.

Blake peered at him from beneath his arm. Will caught his breath. Despite the darkened room, he could see how pale Blake was. His eyes were slits. "Migraine." The word was just about audible.

Oh hell. Will gently lifted Blake's arm away from his eyes. "Okay, tell me. Do you have classic or common migraine?" When Blake's eyes tightened, his brow furrowed, Will tried a different tack. "Do you get visual disturbances, flashing lights, feeling nauseous, or is it just pain?"

Blake's brow cleared a little. "Pain. Dark helps, though." He winced as though pain had suddenly coursed through him.

Okay, common migraine. Will could deal with that. "Have you taken anything for it?"

"Don't have anything with me."

Will thought quickly. "Okay, I'm going to sort you out some painkillers, and then I'm going to help you get rid of it. All right?" Blake gave an almost imperceptible nod. Will got to his feet and slipped from the room into his office, pushing Blake's door shut after him. He picked up his phone and speed-dialled Beth.

"Beth, do you have any of those tablets left that you were taking last week?" Poor Beth had been in agony the previous week with a bad back, and had finally been sent home. Will knew she was taking some pretty strong painkillers. He mentally crossed his fingers.

"Yes, Will, I've got two left in my handbag. Why? You okay?"

Will could have cried with relief. "I'm fine, Blake's not so good. Can I have them?"

"On my way." And she was gone.

Within minutes Beth was at his door, holding out the two capsules and a glass of water. "Is it a migraine?" Will could read the concern in her eyes. "He gets them now and again, but it's been a while."

Will thanked her and after taking the glass and the medication, he went back into Blake's office. He knelt once more on the floor beside Blake.

"Blake, I need you to sit up, just for a second, so you can take some tablets. Are you allergic to anything?

Blake gave out a low moan. "N-no. H-hurts." He struggled to sit upright.

Will's heart went out to him. He knew from past experience the misery migraines could cause, though he'd never had one personally. He sat beside Blake and after placing the glass precariously between his thighs, he put an arm around Blake's shoulder, supporting him. He dropped the capsules into his hand and then reclaimed the glass, watching as Blake took careful mouthfuls. The medication taken, he eased Blake to lie down once more, but after grabbing a cushion and placing it across his lap, he cradled Blake's head on the cushion.

"I'm going to help you, but you'll have to trust me." Blake's only response was a low whimper, but he moved his hand slowly to wrap it around Will's and tighten once. Good enough. "Is the pain in a specific part of your head or is it everywhere?"

"Everywhere," came back the hushed reply. Will had suspected as much. He moved gentle fingers over Blake's scalp, pressing firmly, massaging in circles, never staying in one place for too long. At first Blake stiffened, but then Will felt him sag into the sofa. Will concentrated on his task, applying slight pressure, knowing it would begin to ease the pain.

He lost all track of time. Blake lay quiescent, his head resting on the pillow, his breathing thankfully even. Will eased off on the head massage, now stroking Blake's hair, the movement almost tender. Now and again, he rubbed along Blake's arm and down his back, reassuring him that he wasn't alone. Will had no idea how long he sat like that, but at last Blake stirred, rolling carefully onto his back and looking up at Will in surprise.

"Hi."

Will smiled. "Hi yourself." He kept his voice low. "How's the head?"

Blake became still, as if assessing the situation. "Better."

Will's smile widened. "I'm glad. Now lie there quietly. Let the painkillers do their stuff. Then I'll get you something to eat. That will help, too." Blake blinked several times and opened his mouth, clearly about to protest, but Will laid a single finger across his lips. "No arguments."

Blake closed his eyes for a second and then opened them, giving a slow, careful nod of his head. "Thank you." His eyes closed once more.

Will sat in the darkened room, content to feel Blake's warmth against him. Memories flooded through him. The times he'd held Richard like this, seen that same look of gratitude when the pain left him. Tears pricked his eyelids. He wished Richard could have seen this day. He would have been so proud of Will. He closed his eyes and said a silent prayer of thanks for the man who had turned his life around. Maybe one day Will would get up enough courage to share that part of his life with Blake. Maybe.

Blake groaned. He'd never get them all finished. He stared in exasperation at the monitor, the words no longer registering. How in hell had he gotten so far behind?

"Take a break. Please."

Blake's head jerked up. Will was at their adjoining door, arms full of folders, his eyes fixed on Blake.

Blake snorted. "I don't have *time* for a break. These submissions came in eight weeks ago." Every writer who submitted was given a turn-around time of six to eight weeks to hear if their manuscript had been successful. For reasons he couldn't quite fathom, Blake had fallen behind and now there were eight authors who were already past the deadline. He glanced at his watch. It was five thirty. The office closed officially at four, but he was seldom home before seven. He expelled his breath in one long push of air. There was nothing for it. He'd have to stay and get it done.

He groaned. "Oh fuck. I was supposed to have dinner with Melissa tonight, too." He couldn't miss Will's sardonic grin. He remembered the first time she'd waltzed into the office after Will had begun to work. Melissa had introduced herself as Blake's girlfriend and Will had been momentarily too stunned to respond. Once she'd left, however, the questions began. Will found it most amusing, the sod.

"I'll ring her and cancel. You go on home," he told Will. "I'm going to stay and finish these."

Will frowned. "How many do you have left?" Blake told him. "Can I help?"

Blake sighed. "It's a nice offer, but you know I don't delegate these."

Will persisted. "So you're reading through the story summaries, deciding if it sounds viable and if it does, reading through the manuscript?" Blake nodded. "And if not, they get put on the No Thank You pile?"

Blake smirked. "Inaccurate, but yeah, you've got the general idea."

"And they can't wait until tomorrow?"

Blake shook his head. "We're already over the limit. More than a couple of the authors have emailed to inquire." He stared glumly at the file on his screen. Will hadn't moved. And suddenly Blake relented. *Just this once*, he told himself. "Actually," he began slowly, "you *could* help me."

"Name it."

"Would you read through the summaries? Decide if you think it's a story we'd want to release? Then I'll skim through those that you think suitable."

Something crossed Will's face. Blake cursed inwardly. Of course—Will probably had a client lined up for tonight. In the two months since Will had joined the company, Blake hadn't once brought up the subject. For reasons he didn't want to analyse too deeply, Blake felt uncomfortable at the thought of Will being off somewhere getting fucked. He told himself it was none of his business, as long as Will's work wasn't affected. And he had nothing but praise for that. Will was a treasure. They worked well together, Will often anticipating Blake's requirements before he had the chance to say a word. But that didn't stop the thought which slipped through Blake's brain with disturbing regularity. *Why don't you have another night with him? You* know *you want to.* Wanting was one thing. Following through was another thing entirely. Blake pushed the thought aside. Better to keep things professional—even if his hole clenched tight at the thought of Will fucking him again.

And now he'd clearly put Will in an awkward position. "Look, if that's going to be a problem, then no worries. Go on home."

Will narrowed his lips. "Nah, it's okay. I just have to make a call first, that's all."

Blake nodded, although his chest tightened. Yeah, Will was supposed to be 'working' tonight. *You know, I really didn't want to know that.* "Okay, thank you. You make your call and I'll make us some coffee. Looks like we could use some." Will gave him a brief nod and left the room. Blake stared at the screen, his mind focused not on the information there but on Will. Internally he berated himself. *Why the fuck should it matter to you if he was going to be off fucking some guy tonight?* Blake couldn't account for it. His night with Will still lingered in his memory. Maybe what was required was another call to Jenny. *I need to get laid. After all, it's been two months since....* Yeah. Since Will. Blake scowled. It seemed his mind had a default right now. Every thought path seemed to lead back to his gorgeous PA.

Working with Will was easy. They just got on with it. But that didn't stop him looking at Will every once in a while, usually when he was sure Will was engrossed by a task. Two months hadn't diminished the impact of that first meeting. Blake loved the way Will rubbed his bottom lip when he was deep in thought. Those sexy milk chocolate eyes that Blake could so easily lose himself in. He shook himself. Enough.

"Pizza was a damn good idea."

Blake couldn't agree more. When both their stomachs had started growling, he'd reached for the phone and organized a delivery. The meat lover's pizza had definitely filled a hole, and both men sated, they were back at their task. Blake had to admit, having Will help like this was a godsend. He'd already allocated three authors to the rejection pile. And the one he'd told Blake he must read? Damn, it was good. Not that Blake would make this a regular event. Reading the submissions kept him in touch with things.

Will got up and stretched, his long arms reaching above his head. Blake eyed his lean torso as Will's shirt escaped from his pants, revealing a glimpse of creamy skin. Hurriedly he looked away before Will caught him.

"I'd say we're about done here." He closed down the computer with a sigh. Five contracts to go out the following morning. And three of them for new authors.

"I think they're going to be really good." Will tucked his shirt back into his pants. Blake glanced at his watch. Hell, it was nearly ten. But at least they'd got it done.

"God, my shoulders ache." He rubbed at his right shoulder, trying awkwardly to massage the muscle.

"Here, let me do that." Will came across to stand behind his chair and began to knead Blake's shoulders, his fingers digging into the muscles in a really good way that had Blake groaning.

"Damn, you're good at that."

Will chuckled. "We aim to please."

He worked the tight muscles with his thumbs and Blake dropped his head forward, eyes closed, letting out little whimpers as Will's fingers worked their magic. "Does that feel better?"

Blake moaned softly. "That feels like heaven." Will halted in his task and then Blake caught his breath as Will reached around to the front and slipped his hand under Blake's shirt. He stroked down Blake's chest, rubbing his fingers over Blake's nipple. "Oh fuck," Blake whispered. "God, yes." Will reached down with both hands to unbutton his shirt, and then slid his hands over Blake's chest, Will's touch warm and sensual. He could feel Will's breath against his ear.

"Like that?"

Blake shuddered as Will teased his nipples, which hardened into tight nubs. "Oh, oh God, that's so good." When Will pulled away, he let out a growl—until Will hauled him to his feet and propelled him toward the sofa, pushing him down onto it on his back. Will dropped onto his knees beside him and stared at Blake's face, eyes wide. He stroked Blake's bared chest with one hand.

"Want to kiss you." Will's voice was husky with arousal.

Blake's pulse began to race. "Do it. Kiss me." He reached up and grabbed Will's head, pulling him down roughly until their lips met in a kiss which took his breath away.

He moaned into Will's mouth, the sound swallowed as Will sucked at his tongue. Will slid his hand lower until he reached Blake's pants, and then Blake gasped as the clasp was freed, then the zipper was tugged.

Will never let up kissing him, sliding his agile tongue deep into Blake's mouth even as he wrapped his hand around Blake's dick and tightened around it. Blake whimpered, and Will broke the kiss, only to pull free of Blake's hand and move toward his cock.

"Yes!" Blake hissed as his dick was engulfed in a hot, wet mouth. He hardened instantly as Will began sucking him deeper while he impatiently pulled Blake's pants over his hips. Then he resumed his sensuous task as he grabbed Blake's balls. "Oh shit, Will, I'm not gonna last."

Will let out an evil sounding chuckle around his shaft and then started to hum, the vibrations making everything that much hotter.

All too soon Blake knew he was about to come. He cried out as Will worked his cock with his hand, lips tight around the shaft, his head bobbing faster over Blake's groin. "Close, so close," he stammered out, and then he felt his cock swell in Will's mouth. Will drank him down, sucking the last drop from his dick with little noises that told of his pleasure. Blake lay there shaking as Will cleaned his cock with his tongue, before moving back to kiss him, sharing the last of Blake's come.

They kissed, this time more languidly, Blake's fingers moving gently through Will's short hair, their lips soft against each other. Blake wondered at the image he must have presented: chest bared, pants pushed roughly down to mid-thigh, his spent cock lying limply against his thigh. Will released his mouth with a sigh.

"You taste delicious."

Blake felt the flush which rose up from his chest and neck, finally reaching his cheeks. "And you're wicked."

Will chuckled. "Didn't hear you complaining, though."

Blake snorted. "What man in his right mind *complains* about a kick-ass blow-job?"

Will preened. "Glad to know my oral skills are appreciated." He got up from the floor and held out a hand to Blake who sat up, fastening up his shirt.

"Thank you, by the way," he said sincerely. Will's eyebrows lifted. "For staying, I mean. I really do appreciate it. And especially for what just took place." Blake's cheeks reddened. "I'm sure you must have had a client booked for this evening, so I'll reimburse you what you would have made tonight. I wouldn't want you to be out of pocket."

Will froze. His eyes narrowed. The cold expression on his face made Blake's heart stutter in his chest. "Will? What have I said?"

Will locked eyes with him. He stared at Blake in silence for so long that Blake started to worry.

"Thank you very much. You just made me feel like a whore." The words were delivered in a flat tone, but Blake saw him swallow, saw a shiver ripple through him.

Blake's jaw dropped, his eyes growing wide. "What?" He didn't understand.

Will's jaw clenched. "You don't have a fucking clue what I had planned for tonight. And by saying that, you made it sound like that's all I do. Fuck guys." He gritted out the words. "Well, fuck you." Will got up off the sofa and strode into his office, slamming the door shut behind him.

Blake paled. He got to his feet and hurried to the adjoining door. When he opened it, Will was putting on his suit jacket and picking up his keys. "Oh God, Will, I didn't mean to... I'm sorry..." Will ignored him. He stood there trembling as his computer shut itself down. Blake approached him slowly. "Will. Please, don't go. Please. I'm so sorry." His heart was beating fast. *Oh God, tell me I've not just fucked this up beyond repair.* He watched Will become still. Long seconds passed.

At last Will looked him in the eye. "Just so you know—not that it's any of your fucking business—tonight I was supposed to be at the LGBT youth shelter in Charing Cross. I go there once a week and hang out with the kids. We play pool, watch TV, chat mostly." He stared resolutely at Blake. "You don't know me, Mr. Davis."

Blake wasn't going to stop, not now Will was speaking to him. "Then come back to the sofa, sit down, and talk to me. *Tell* me." Will's jaw was still clenched. "*Please*, Will." He could have wept with relief when Will finally nodded, and the two men went back to Blake's sofa. Will sagged against the cushions, Blake sitting beside him. For a moment neither of them spoke. Will stared up at the ceiling as he finally started to speak.

"You don't know the whole story," Will began. "So maybe I should explain something which might make it a little easier." He shook himself. "Christ, I swore I was never gonna let you know *any* of this, but.... When I took on the job at J's, it *was* as an escort. I escort a lot of women to functions, balls, stuff like that. They feel safer knowing they're with a gay guy who isn't going to hit on them at the end of the night."

"I can understand that." Blake couldn't take his eyes off Will. The man had a haunted expression about his face. Will scrubbed his hand over his cheek.

"Then about a month before you and I..." Will flushed and cleared his throat. "A month before your birthday, Jenny asked me if I would consider doing a little more than just escorting. It didn't take me long to work out she meant sex. For reasons I'm not about to go into right now, I wasn't keen on the idea, not even remotely—until she mentioned what I would be earning. Let's just say it was a lot more." His eyes met Blake's for the first time in what was obviously a painful confession. "I said yes." The words were whispered. Blake reached across and grabbed hold of his hand, holding it tightly. Will gave him a grateful look before continuing with his story, his voice growing steadier.

"Well, a few weeks went by and I carried on as an escort. I tried not to think about what I'd agreed to do. Until one day Jenny rings me up and asks how I would feel about having sex with this really nice guy by the name of Blake."

Blake stared. "I was your first client?" Will nodded. "Wow. And there was me thinking you must have been doing this for a while, you were so confident and assured. I'd never have guessed."

Rather than look pleased at Blake's words, Will seemed very unhappy. He pulled his hand free of Blake's and got up, picking up his jacket from where he'd dropped it by the sofa.

"I think I'm going to go home now. I'll see you tomorrow." His voice was tight. Blake watched in dismay as Will exited the office, not looking back once.

Blake was at a loss. He sat there thinking back on Will's tale. There was much more to his PA than he'd thought, and Blake suspected there was even more to come.

That's if he comes back to work for you to find out. He couldn't shut out the thought. The mood Will was in, Blake wouldn't be surprised to see his resignation the following morning. Blake flushed with shame for making Will feel so cheap. The young man was no whore, that much was evident. Blake decided there and then to make it up to Will—if he ever got the chance.

CHAPTER SIX

Will didn't want to go to work.

He lay in his bed, staring at his alarm clock where the minutes ticked away, already past the point where he should have been up, showered and dressed. Not that he'd needed the alarm this morning. He estimated he'd had about two hours sleep, off and on. All the way home from the office the night before, he'd mentally kicked himself for coming onto Blake in the first place. Why in hell hadn't he just kept his hands to himself?

'Cause my boss is hot and I wanted him. Duh. Will had been fighting his attraction to Blake since day one. And he knew full well why he'd let go last night. He'd wanted to know if Blake would respond when he wasn't paying for it. *Well, I got my answer, didn't I?* The noises and whimpers coming from Blake had gone straight to his dick. And as for the taste of him... Will had almost come from watching his boss trembling as he came into Will's mouth. Then Blake had gone and ruined it.

You know *he was sorry.* Yeah, Will knew. It didn't make the thought of facing his boss that morning any easier. At least Blake knew now.

The sound of a horn in the street below broke through his reveries. It was no use. He'd have to face Blake sooner or later. Later sounded pretty good right now.

Will smelled the coffee as soon as he came through the main door. The clock above Karen's desk showed eight ten. Will wondered what Blake was making of his late arrival. Then it hit him. *He might think I'm not coming in at all.* Will went swiftly to his office, took off his greatcoat and hung it up, before knocking quietly on the adjoining door.

62

"Come in." Blake sounded subdued, even through a closed door. Will pushed it open. Blake was seated at his desk, a mug of coffee next to him. He looked up and his eyes became large and round. "You're... you're here." There was no mistaking the look of relief in those gorgeous blue eyes. Before Will had time to utter a word, Ed appeared behind him with a mug of coffee. He thrust it into Will's hand, almost spilling its contents in the process.

"Mornin'. Was it you who pissed 'im off, then?" Typical Ed, no beating about the bush. "'Cos I tell ya, if it was, yer gonna answer to me." Ed looked ready to lay into Will. In that instant Will could have hugged the man. Ed was staunchly loyal to Blake and would always have his back. Will knew from conversations with Blake that Ed had been the first member of staff that he'd taken on six years ago, and that the two of them had seen through the drastic changes Blake had seen fit to implement when he'd taken over the company.

Will looked across at Blake, who was watching the interaction between the two men with trepidation. Will decided to go with honesty.

"Yeah, Ed, some of it's down to me, that's true, but I'd say both parties are at fault here."

He met Blake's eyes. Blake stared at him for a few seconds before nodding. Ed clearly noted Blake's reaction. His hands, which had been clenched into fists, relaxed.

"Okay, then sort it out, the pair of ya." Ed glared at both of them, waiting until both men acknowledged him before withdrawing from the room.

"Come in and close the door," Blake told him. Will complied and then stood, mug in hand, feeling distinctly awkward. Blake gestured toward the sofa and Will walked across to sit down. Blake looked down at his desk and Will's stomach churned. The silence was killing him.

Blake opened his mouth to speak and Will held up a hand to stop him. Blake's brow furrowed.

"Look, before you say anything," Will began, "I'm sorry for the abrupt way I left here last night. That was rude." And it wasn't Blake's fault. His boss had no idea why his last remark was received so badly. "You apologized, after all."

"Yeah, and then I went and said something else to upset you." Blake spoke quietly. "I can't tell you how that makes me feel, Will. I hurt you last night—not once but twice. I can only ask you to forgive me, and to accept my promise that I will try to make it up to you somehow. I don't want to lose you."

Will could see the pain in his eyes. Blake wasn't angry with him—Blake was obviously unhappy about causing Will any pain. Okay, so he meant not losing Will from his company: Will wasn't naive enough to think anything different.

But it was clear to Will that Blake cared. Any residual ill feeling he might still have borne toward his boss melted in that instant. A memory of Richard flashed through Will's mind. Here was another genuinely caring man who Will felt compelled to trust. For the second time in his life, Will wanted to share with another human being.

"Listen, there's something I'd like you to do for me."

Blake's brow cleared. "What?"

Will got up and went back into his office to retrieve his briefcase. He pulled out a USB flash drive and handed it to Blake. Blake took it, looking puzzled.

"There's a novel on this that I'd like you to read."

Blake stared at the black metallic flash drive. The crease between his eyes deepened. "A novel?"

Will nodded. "Yeah. When you've read it, we can talk some more." He gave Blake a feeble smile. "But right now I need to get on and organize your calendar so you know what you're doing from one day to the next." He turned to go to his office, but as he reached the door, Blake's words stopped him.

"Aren't you going to tell me who wrote it?"

Will turned back to him. "I did." And without waiting to see Blake's reaction, he left the room.

Will cuddled up to his pillow, inhaling the aroma of fresh, clean sheets. He always loved that just-washed smell. It was even better in the summer when he could take advantage of the weather to dry everything on the line which stretched out on the rooftop of his apartment building. And of course there was another advantage to laundry days—laying down a towel on the ground behind the billowing sheets and stretching out on it on the nude, letting his body soak up the sun's rays. Heaven. Sheer heaven.

He glanced at the clock. Nearly one in the morning and he still couldn't sleep. He knew why, of course. Ever since he'd given Blake the novel that morning, he'd done nothing but think about it. The day seemed to crawl by. Throughout his meetings with Lizzie, Peter and Rick, during his lunch break—*C'mon, let's face it*, he told himself, *every fucking minute*—his thoughts had never strayed far from Blake. Was he reading it right now? Did he love it? Hate it? Round and round his thoughts went, like a hamster on a wheel. He was really going out on a limb here. Entrusting Blake with the book was *huge*.

Beside him on the bedside table, his phone vibrated. Will frowned. Who the hell was texting him at this hour? He glanced at the screen—Blake.

You awake?

Smiling, Will hit speed dial. "No, I was asleep. Your text woke me up." He heard the hitch in Blake's breath and snorted. "I'm kidding. Why aren't you asleep? You're not still working, are you?" His boss badly needed to get some work-life balance going.

There was a pause before Blake spoke. "I couldn't put it down."

Oh. Oh wow. Will was momentarily stunned.

"Bloody hell, Will, it's... it's..." Silence. "Will, it's damn good."

Will suddenly felt about ten feet tall. Warmth flooded through him. He'd poured so much into the book.

"I have to ask. Is this all your imagination, or is it based on a real person? Because the main character, Terry..." Will swallowed. "Oh my God, Will, the life he led. It had me crying into my pillow. And when Donald found him, and took him in...." Will heard something that sounded suspiciously like a sob. Oh fuck. Blake was crying.

Will waited until Blake's breathing was more controlled before he spoke. "Yes, it's based on a real person." He swallowed heavily, unable to believe what he was about to say. "Terry is me, Blake." Silence. Will waited anxiously. "Blake?" Long seconds ticked by.

At last he heard noise at the other end. A sniffle. Deep breathing.

"Now I understand. It all makes sense. Will, thank you. Thank you for trusting me enough to let me read it."

Will's heart soared to hear those words. No condemnation. No disgust. Just acceptance.

"Can you tell me some more? I want to hear it."

Fuck. Will froze, unsure of how to react. It had been a long time since he'd told his tale. Writing the book had been hard enough. It opened up wounds he'd thought long since healed, making everything fresh and raw once more. Blake said nothing but Will could hear his breathing, steadier now. Will came to a decision. He switched the phone to speaker phone, cuddled the pillow tighter and began to speak.

"When I was fifteen, I made a huge mistake. I came out to my parents. If I'd known how they would react, I would have kept my mouth shut." He closed his eyes. The pain never left him.

"They took it badly?"

"They threw me out." He couldn't miss Blake's sharp intake of breath. Will clamped down on the surge of grief which flowed through him. "So there I was, homeless, no relatives to speak of. I quit going to school—I mean, what was the point?—and I found myself living on the streets, faced with the task of surviving."

"You really were a rent boy?"

Will nodded, until he remembered that Blake couldn't see him. "Yes. I used to hang out by the adult bookstore. It wasn't that difficult to get picked up there, especially looking as young as I did." His chest tightened as he remembered. No, there'd been no shortage of men eager to fuck an underage boy. He shivered. "I used to try to find guys who'd take me home for the night. And if that wasn't possible, I used to sleep in an abandoned warehouse on the docks. Well, me and a few other derelicts."

"Were... were you safe?"

Will could have kissed the man for his concern. "Always. No condom, no fuck. Not even a blow-job." He still couldn't believe he was telling Blake all this. The strange thing was it felt right to share it with him.

"How long did you live like that?"

Will shivered. "For about a year. By then I'd found a shelter for homeless gay kids, run by this older guy, Richard." An iron band tightened around his chest.

"Richard's son was gay, but he ran away from home when Richard reacted badly to his coming out. Richard never saw him again." Will could still hear Richard sobbing, late into the night in his room, his sorrow and guilt for what he'd done never leaving him. "He started up the shelter for kids who were in the same situation."

"And then you came along." Will could hear the warmth in Blake's voice.

"Richard said once that he could always spot potential. I think a lot of it was that I reminded him of his son." Will had seen the photos. He and Philip could have been twins. "Anyway, Richard took me in, gave me a home." For which Will would forever be grateful. He'd been suspicious at first—come on, an older guy taking in a sixteen-year-old

rent boy—but Richard had soon allayed his fears. He'd been horrified
to hear Will's story, and had wanted to make things better for him. Will
had come to care deeply for him.

"You moved in with him?"

"Yep. His spare room became my room. He left Philip's room
exactly as it was. I guess he always hoped Philip would return one day."
His heart stuttered briefly. Maybe things might have been different
then. There was no doubt losing his son took its toll on Richard's
health.

"Richard gave me a roof over my head and fed and clothed me. He
sent me to a school to take my exams. I'd always been a bright kid, and
boy, was I thankful for that. I had some serious catching-up to do."

Encouraged by Will's academic success, Richard had encouraged
him to get a degree, and had offered to pay for his studies, but there was
no way Will would accept that. He'd gone down the route of student
loans instead, which wasn't nearly enough, so he'd got a job working in
a fast food restaurant. He wanted to pay Richard back in some way, but
the older man was bloody stubborn.

"I'll bet Richard was really proud of you."

Will stifled a sob. "Two years into my degree, Richard died of a
heart attack. He never got to see me graduate." It was no use. The tears
started to flow.

"Will, it's okay." Blake spoke softly. "Let it out, babe."

Will caught his breath at the endearment. It felt good. No, it felt
better than good.

"I'm okay," he said shakily. He wiped his tears on the sheet and
took a breath. "So suddenly I was homeless again. I moved into student
accommodation, but that meant more expense. I needed more money
to live on, so I made the decision—I went back to being a rent boy."
Will didn't want to think about those years. Life got scary. "When I
graduated, I got a job with Willetts, a small publishing house. It was
a fair salary, I suppose, but it barely made a dent in my debts. Until

one night about five months ago, when this guy who picked me up got talking about J's. He thought I'd be perfect for them. And the rest, you know."

Will listened to Blake breathing steadily. "My God, Will, what a story. Never mind that—what a book! You're an exceptional writer." Will glowed at these words. "Let me publish it."

Will became still. He hadn't shown Blake the book for that reason. And now he couldn't believe Blake's reaction. He was kidding—right? "Are you serious?" The words crept out.

"Of course I'm serious!" Will could hear the note of excitement in Blake's voice. "It'll be a hit, mark my words." There was a pause. "You could dedicate it to Richard's memory. And you might also consider donating some of your royalties to that shelter where you go once a week. I'm sure they'd appreciate any extra funding."

Will loved that. What he loved even more was that Blake had come up with the idea in the first place. A quick glance at the clock shocked him. It was already gone two.

"I think we both need to sleep." He chuckled. "We can discuss this in the morning."

"Will, how can you expect me to sleep now? I'm way too keyed to sleep." Will could hear it. A wicked thought crossed his mind.

"What're you wearing?" He grinned to himself.

"What?" He could hear Blake's puzzlement.

"What are you wearing? Pyjamas? Boxers? Briefs?" Will lowered his voice, making it husky. "Nothing?"

"Oh, you have *got* to be kidding me." Will snickered. *Come on, Blake, play along...* "Okay... briefs." Yeah, now they were in business. Will rolled onto his back and stuffed pillows under his head, the phone resting on the empty pillow next to his head. He was *definitely* going to need to be hands free for what he had in mind.

"Tighty whiteys? Kind of old fashioned but still damn sexy." He tried to picture Blake in his underwear. His cock hardened. Will slipped his hand below the sheet and palmed his dick.

"Black. Tight." Will could hear Blake's breathing speed up slightly. "And getting tighter." *Yes.* Time to have some fun.

"*Ohhh*...you turned on, big boy? You ever done anything like this. Phone sex?"

"Never." There was a pause. "Fuck, Will...." The words were whispered. Will loved the edge of anticipation that was evident in Blake's voice. He reached into his drawer for the lube and slicked up his palm. And then he reached for his Fleshjack.

"But you want to do this, don't you, Blake? This and more?"

"Fuck, yeah." Blake whimpered. "Keep going." That whimper went straight to Will's dick. He pushed his dick through his slick, tight fist, his breathing growing more erratic.

"I'm totally nude. Don't have a stitch of clothing on. And hard. Very hard." And getting harder by the second.

"Oh *fuck*, I can picture you.... Where are you? How hard, baby?" Will liked that. Baby.

"I'm stretched out on my bed. Silk sheets feel so nice on my bare arse. Lights turned low. I'm totally erect. Eight inches and standing straight up. A tiny puddle of pre-come at the tip." Will watched the slender thread of pre-come glisten in the lamplight.

"Wish I was there to taste you. Taste yourself for me." Oh, Blake was definitely getting into this.

"What would you do? Slide between my legs and kiss my dick? Or pull out your cock and make me suck it?" The memory of Blake's dick in his mouth, the taste of him, was suddenly so vivid that Will caught his breath.

"I want to be between your legs. Want to kiss all along the length of your cock." Blake gave out a low moan. "Oh God, I want you in my mouth *so* bad."

Will whimpered as an image flashed through his mind. Blake on his bed, lying on his belly, Will's hard shaft sliding into that beautiful mouth, watching those soft lips around it.

"I can feel your mouth on my balls. Your warm breath blowing against them. Then your tongue sliding up the underside of my dick. Your lips on the head."

"*Yes!*" The sibilant sound was harsh.

"Can you taste my pre-come?" Will's hips started to rock up from the bed.

"Yeah, it's almost sweet. More, baby." Blake's plaintive whine made Will grin.

"Swallow my shaft. Wrap your lips around it. I can feel your tongue caressing it. I'm stroking myself, Blake. Touching myself, imagining it's your mouth sucking me off." Will's hips sped up as he listened to the breathless sounds at the other end of the phone. "Feels amazing. You suck my cock so good. Your tongue is amazing. God, I am *so* turned on. I'm leaking so much. I'm close to shooting. So close." Will struggled to hold on.

"Don't want you to come in my mouth." Brief silence, save for the sound of Blake's harsh breathing. "I want...." Whispered.

"Tell me what you want. Don't be afraid. *Tell* me."

"Want you... want you... to fuck me."

Will had to pull hard on his balls not to come on the spot. "You want to ride me?"

"Fuck, yes. God, Will, I'm so fucking hard right now." Blake moaned, the sound low and full of urgent need.

"I want that too. Can't promise I'll last long once I'm inside. Get yourself ready, Blake." Will grabbed the Fleshjack and dribbled lube into it.

"Yes...fuck, wait!" Will heard a drawer opening and closing. Blake's eager voice had him ready to shoot his load right now. Will breathed deeply, trying to stave off his imminent climax.

"What? I can't wait much longer." Never a truer word spoken.

"My fingers are in my arse." Oh, and wasn't *that* something to picture? Will could see Blake, legs spread, fingers wedged inside that tight hole. This was going to be over *so* quickly.

"Yeah, stretch yourself good."

"Oh fuck, three now... that, that burns.... feels so good."

Will whimpered at the thought. "My cock is lubed up for you. Ready and waiting." Along with his Fleshjack.

"Yes, Will. Ready."

"I can picture you climbing on the bed. Squatting over me, my cock aimed at your hole." Yeah, Will could picture it, all right.

Blake whimpered. "Keep going, baby."

"Lower yourself over me, keep going... lower. Feel my cock pushing at your hole. Relax. Relax. Let me in." Will pushed his cock into the Fleshjack, his hips rocking up almost immediately. He was so close.

"You feel so big. Fuck, yes, Will... Don't stop, don't you dare stop." Blake was panting.

Will thrust up into the Fleshjack. "I'm driving up into you. Arching my hips to impale myself in your arse. All. The. Way." Hips pumped. Faster.

"Oh *fuck*!" Blake cried out. "Fuck me, oh Christ, fuck me!"

"Feel my cock pulsating against your gland? Feel me fucking you hard? Slamming into you again and again? Christ, Blake, I'm gonna come." Will's hips pistoned as he fucked up into the Fleshjack, feeling that familiar tingle at the base of his spine. Not long now.

"Right there! *Oh*!"

The long, drawn-out sound of pure ecstasy was too much. Will started to come, back arching up from the bed. "Fuck yeah! I'm shooting. Fuck, Blake, *fuckfuckfuck*..."

"Oh God, coming, coming so fucking hard! *Will*!" Will lay there, the only sounds Blake's laboured breathing, blending with his own. He listened as Blake gained control of himself once more. "Oh my God. That was...."

"Incredible. That was incredible." Will had never experienced phone sex like it. He pulled off the Fleshjack and grabbed some tissues to wipe his softening cock, hissing as he touched the sensitized head. He dropped the tissues onto the floor along with the Fleshjack. It could wait until morning. "Now go to sleep, Blake."

"Thank you." Will could hear Blake's fatigue. "G'night, Will."

"Night, babe." Both phone and lamp were switched off. Will's last conscious thought before sleep took him was that he badly wanted Blake in his arms right now.

CHAPTER SEVEN

"Oh, not again." Will muttered under his breath at the sight of the chocolate chip muffin sitting in the middle of his desk. Rick was passing by his office door and obviously heard him. He came up quietly behind Will and peered at the object of Will's attention.

"Let me guess—from Karen." Rick smirked.

Will groaned. "God, does *everyone* know about this?"

Rick laughed. "Pretty much, yeah. We're all placing bets as to how long it takes you to cave in and surrender." He eyed the muffin hungrily. "Although it *does* look delicious. *I* should be so lucky, having a sexy lady make me presents of chocolaty goodness every day." He winked.

Will snorted. Sexy? "I swear, I'm not giving her any reason to think she's in with a chance, honest."

Rick guffawed. "Yeah, we can see that, too." He winked once more. "You could always take her on one date and then break it off. You know, make her think you're a total bitch."

Will's eyebrows arched and Rick reddened. More than once, Will had gotten a vibe from the young man, but he wasn't about to test his theory. "Well, if you like the look of the muffin so much, *you* have it." He picked it up and thrust it at Rick, who grinned.

"Yay! Thanks, Will, you're a sweetie." Rick gave him a gleeful look and exited the room quickly, hiding his prize in his hands. Will had to laugh. He really liked the exuberant Rick, who was always laughing and joking. Not to mention the fact that he was a real cutie.

He walked over to the adjoining door which was closed. Oh really. Will suddenly knew *exactly* why Blake had shut it. In the last two weeks, he'd caught Blake three times. He grasped the handle and quietly pushed the door open. Putting his head around the door, he grinned as he caught sight of Blake at his desk, his attention totally focused on the monitor. Earbuds prevented him from hearing Will's approach as Will crept stealthily toward him. At the last minute, Blake jerked his head up, hastily pulling the earphones loose and blushing guiltily.

"Again? You not got enough work to do?" Will tutted, but he knew his twitching lips gave the game away. Blake's hand moved to the mouse. "Stop right there." Will forced as much authority into his voice as he could. He vividly remembered the effect he'd had on Blake during his birthday encounter. Blake definitely had submissive tendencies. Well, Will could let out his inner Dom at the drop of a hat. Blake's hand froze, hovering over the mouse.

Will moved around the desk to see what claimed his boss's attention. He let out a long, low whistle. Blake was watching an orgy scene. At least seven or eight men, their bodies oiled up and glistening, were engaged in varied sexual acts. The camera focused on the men in the forefront who were having a threesome, two spit roasting the third.

Will chortled. "Like what you see?" He glanced down at Blake's crotch and snorted. Fuck, the man was tenting. Blake gazed up at him, eyes glazed with lust.

"I was imagining what it would feel like to be the meat in *that* sandwich." His eyes gleamed. Blake let out a low moan as he rubbed his erection with the heel of his hand. The sight had Will stiffening instantly. Inwardly he groaned. Why did his boss have to look so downright *fuckable*? Since their phone sex two weeks previously, he'd dreamed frequently about Blake, and the dreams were always the same—erotic.

His dick hardened further as he watched Blake slowly palm his erection, eyes fixed not on the screen but on Will. Oh, Blake wanted to play, did he? The way Will was feeling right now, Blake might get more than he bargained for. Because Will had a wicked idea.

"Got any condoms on you, Blake?"

Blake's hand froze in mid rub. "W-what?" He watched as Will walked slowly across to his office door and locked it. *What the fuck?* Then he locked the adjoining door. "Will? What are you doing?" he hissed.

"Answer the question." God, when Will spoke to him like that, all the blood rushed south. Blake flushed hot and cold at the same time.

"I always keep a condom in my briefcase. For emergencies." He swallowed as Will's eyes gleamed, a wicked light in them.

"Get it."

Oh my God, he's not thinking of.... Blake was suddenly so hard he ached. Okay, so he'd fantasized once or twice about Will fucking him at work, the likelihood of being caught sending frissons of excitement skating up and down his spine, but now that he was faced with the very real possibility of it actually happening.... Fingers trembling, he reached into his briefcase and extracted the foil wrapped condom, giving it a cursory glance to check its expiration date. Phew. Still viable.

Will grinned when he saw it. "Okay, clear your desk. Now."

Blake gulped. Oh hell. Hurriedly he began to pick up the folders which lay strewn across his desk and drop them hastily onto the floor. All that remained was the keyboard and monitor. Will moved stealthily toward him, unbuttoning his fly and taking out his cock, pulling at it leisurely. Fuck, he was hard. Blake shivered as Will came to stand behind him, so close that Blake could feel heat pouring off him. Will reached around his waist to undo his fly, and then Blake's pants were pulled down roughly, baring his arse. Blake gasped as Will stroked a finger along his crease.

"Jacket off."

The deep, rich voice had Blake obeying him instantly. He shucked off the jacket impatiently and stood trembling as Will slid warm hands up under his shirt, stroking his back, before reaching around to tug and twist his nipples. God, did he remember *all* Blake's hot spots? Blake let out a low mewl.

"Uh-uh, baby." Will's breath fluttered against his ear. "You can't make a sound. Someone might hear."

Blake's heart gave a jolt as his hair was grabbed, forcing his head back as Will claimed his mouth in a brutal kiss, all teeth and tongue, just what he wanted. Will's tongue plundered his mouth relentlessly. And then that finger was back, sliding over his hole. Will broke the kiss and Blake made a soft noise of disappointment. Will chuckled.

"We're gonna need lube. Don't really want to fuck you dry."

Oh hell. Blake fucking *loved* it when a partner talked dirty.

"In... in my bathroom. There's some hand lotion." He stammered out the words.

Another chuckle resounded in his ear. "Uh-uh. Not good. Doesn't work so well with condoms. Where's your Vaseline lip balm?" Will had seen him use it once or twice. Blake pointed shakily to the top drawer of his desk. Will scrummaged around in the drawer, pouncing on it eagerly. "Lemon flavoured? Nice." Blake hadn't dared move. He stood there, pants around his thighs, his shirt half covering his arse, cock poking out from below it, hard and wanting. Will stood beside him, slowly undoing his tie. Blake swallowed. The look in those brown eyes....

"Take off your tie."

Hands shaking, Blake obeyed. He held it out to Will. "Good boy." Blake shivered at the words. Fuck. One night of hot sex nearly three months ago and yet Will remembered *everything*. He held himself still as Will came up behind him.

"Close your eyes, baby." Blake closed them, shuddering as he felt the silk tie cover his eyes, tightening around his head as Will tied it at the back of his head.

He trembled as those intrepid hands once more caressed his bare skin under his shirt—and then stifled a gasp as the shirt was pulled off his shoulders, his arms freed.

"Hands behind your back." Those short, sexy instructions ramped up his arousal. He let out a low cry as his hands were seized around the wrists and tied together with his shirt, not tight enough to cut off circulation but enough to prevent him freeing himself. Will grabbed the bundled shirt and pushed him over the desk, his face meeting the smooth grain of the varnished wood, belly resting on the edge of the desk.

"Ready to be fucked?" The words were delivered quietly, but with real heat behind them. Blake did his best to bob his head, but it was difficult—Will pushed him flat, hand pressing against the center of his back below his nape, between his shoulder blades.

"Yes, oh fuck, yes," Blake whispered. He was at Will's mercy—and he fucking loved it.

"Hmmm, not quite ready. We need something else." Blake moaned as another tie covered his mouth, gagging him. He whimpered as Will tied it at the back of his head. Oh God. Still half dressed, blindfolded, bound and gagged—it was all his fantasies brought to life.

That hand was back at his nape, holding him immobile. The faint aroma of lemon suddenly filled his nose. Will had opened the lip balm. Blake shivered as the light scent filled his senses. A stray thought filtered through his brain. *God, every time I use it from now on, I'm going to think of this.* Blake liked that. The thought was driven from him as two fingers plunged into his arse. *Fuck...*

Will bent low over him, his shirt soft against Blake's cool skin. "Going to fuck you now, baby." His breath tickled Blake's ear. Blake's cry was muffled by the gag as Will twisted his fingers deep inside him, finger-fucking him roughly. Blake pushed back, desperate for what was coming. Will kissed down his spine, never pausing once in his erotic assault. "God, you're eager, aren't you?" Blake mewled. Will let out a soft laugh. "Patience. I want this arse ready for when I slide eight inches of hard, thick cock into it." Blake whimpered. *Come on and* fuck *me already*. "Going to let go of you while I put on the condom. Don't move."

Blake bobbed his head in frantic agreement as Will released him, his fingers pulling free of his body. The sound of the foil seemed so loud. He heard the snap of latex and shivered in anticipation. He lay absolutely still, never daring to move, listening for every sound, waiting anxiously for the first sign that he was about to get fucked. At last he felt Will's cock, hot and hard as he pressed against his hole. He pushed back but Will held him down.

"No, baby. *I'm* in charge here." Blake could have screamed in frustration. He held himself still, listening for any sound—and then his body went rigid as Will thrust into him, filling him completely. *Fuck, he's big.* Will grabbed him at the wrists and shoulder as he slammed into him, balls slapping against Blake's arse. Blake's mouth opened in a silent scream, the sound cut off by the gag as Will assaulted his arse, pushing him relentlessly toward orgasm.

"Fuck, I'd forgotten how tight you are." Will moved faster now, his cock hitting his gland with every thrust.

Blake's dick lay trapped against the desk, sliding over the smooth wood as each thrust propelled him forward. He whimpered in gratitude as Will released his shoulder and pulled at his hips, lifting his arse higher. Then he reached around and grabbed Blake's cock, tugging at it forcefully, the action just the right side of painful.

"You gonna come for me soon?" Will panted above him. Blake could feel the scrape of Will's belt buckle against the back of his thighs, his shirt flapping against his back. God, he wished he could see how this looked. Will fully clothed, fucking him over his desk, Blake half bare, pants halfway down his legs. The image took him perilously close to the edge, and he shuddered. Will sped up, hips slamming into Blake as he withdrew almost entirely, only to thrust back into him repeatedly. It was too much. Blake's balls pulled up tight against his body.

Will's chest met his back, his hips pumping as he fucked him hard, his fist a grip of iron around Blake's cock. "Come for me."

Blake stiffened as he shot his load, listening to Will's breathless pants as he fucked him through his orgasm, Blake's internal muscles tightening around his dick. Suddenly Will's cock felt bigger, filling him completely, and he knew Will was coming. Will grabbed him around his chest, holding him tightly against his body as he came. Blake felt the pulse of his come deep inside him, its heat muted by the latex. Will lay prone, their bodies joined, Will's cock held prisoner within him.

Blake could have cried with relief as Will thoughtfully removed his gag and blindfold, before untying the shirt from around his wrists.

He rubbed at Blake's wrists, encouraging blood flow, and then took hold of his head to turn it toward him and bring their lips together in a kiss which was sublimely tender. Blake lost himself in the kiss, desperate to hold onto the connection between them, mewling with disappointment as their lips parted company.

"Oh babe." Will's voice shook with emotion. "That was wonderful."

Blake let out a soft entreaty. "Kiss me." Will seemed only too happy to oblige, claiming his mouth immediately, their kisses intense and heady. He felt Will's softened cock slip from his body.

The sound of the door handle rattling was an unwelcome intrusion.

"It's locked, remember?" Will whispered. Blake nodded in relief, only to have his heart give a jolt as he heard a familiar voice on the other side of the door.

"Have you seen Blake? His office appears to be locked." *Oh fuck.* Melissa.

Will's eyes widened and they separated frantically, Will yanking off the condom and disposing of it hastily, the pair of them pulling up pants, rapidly dressing themselves, and all the while they could hear Rick outside, talking with Melissa. Blake glanced around in a panic. The air was thick with the scent of come and sex. Will dashed into the bathroom and emerged with the air freshener, spraying it around wildly. Blake's fingers refused to cooperate as he tried to retie his tie, his heart giving another jolt as the handle rattled once more.

"Blake? Are you in there?" Her nasal voice sounded so loud.

Will placed his folders back on the desk, before glancing down swiftly at himself and then Blake, giving him the thumbs up. Blake went to the door and with a final hand through his hair to calm it, turned the key and opened the door. Melissa halted in mid action, clearly about to knock. Rick was standing beside her, looking very apologetic.

"Melissa. What can I do for you?" He tried his best to keep his tone even.

Melissa pushed past him and strode into the room, scanning it, clearly suspicious. "Why was the door locked?" Her voice was hard.

Blake arched his brows. "We were in the middle of a planning session. I'd asked for us not to be disturbed." He scowled. He hated the way she turned up unannounced, walking into the office as if she had a God given right to be there. Maybe it was time to put paid to this whim of his father's. No way would Blake come out, but he'd make sure Justin knew he wouldn't put up with having any more would-be girlfriends foisted upon him.

Melissa walked over to the desk, teetering in those ridiculous four-inch heels. Her long, red hair was as immaculately groomed as ever, her make-up impeccable. Blake sighed internally. Melissa's appearance was her number one priority. He moved toward her, about to ask her to leave when she froze, her attention fixed on the desk. Oh hell. Now what? Then she walked over to the waste-paper bin and glanced down into it. Blake saw Will's face pale.

Melissa turned slowly on her heel to face him. "Well, that explains a lot." There was a cold, malicious smile across her face.

Will stood frozen to the spot by the sofa. *Oh fuck.* This was going to be bad.

Melissa had her back to him, her attention focused on Blake. Will moved quietly across to the desk, but she whirled around to glare at him. "And you can stay right where you are." She smiled, revealing perfectly even, white teeth, but there was no warmth to her smile. Without moving her head, she barked an instruction to Blake. "Close the door, Blake. We don't want to be disturbed, do we? Not while the three of us have a little chat." She winked at Will, who couldn't help the shudder that rippled through him. He couldn't take his eyes off her, dimly hearing Blake close the door and cross the room to the sofa.

"Why don't you sit down, Will?" Her voice sent a shiver down his spine. "And Blake, come sit next to your boyfriend."

Blake's face was deathly pale. "W-what are you talking about?"

Melissa's lips narrowed. "Don't bother to deny it. There are spots of come on your desk and a condom wrapper in your bin—along with the used condom." Blake's eyes met his. Will could only shrug helplessly. He knew what she'd seen as soon as she'd glanced at the contents of the bin. Blake sat down heavily on the sofa. Will couldn't help his response: he reached out and took his hand, holding it tight. Blake glanced down and then gave him a grateful look.

"Oh, how sweet."

Both men turned to face her. Melissa's cheeks were flushed, but the expression on her face was pure spite.

Blake straightened. "What do you want?" Will was proud of him.

"Nothing much." Somehow Will doubted that. "I've had enough of being the latest in a long line of unsuccessful girlfriends, that's all."

"So?" Blake's forehead creased. Will was as confused by the statement as he was.

"So, I want to be Mrs. Blake Davis." Melissa smiled.

Will's heart sank. She had to be fucking kidding. He glanced across at Blake to gauge his reaction. Blake stared at her.

"What on earth makes you think I'd marry *you*?" he retorted, clearly no longer bothering to mask his emotions. "And why would you want to marry someone who's gay?"

Melissa stared at him, eyes glacial. "Because if you don't, I'll make sure *Daddy* dearest finds out exactly what his son gets up to with his handsome PA." There were those perfect teeth again. "And you can kiss goodbye to running this company. I can't see Justin Davis letting a *fag* have control of his precious Trinity Publishing. Can *you*?" She eyed Blake appreciatively. "And as for why I'd marry you, I read the papers. I know Trinity is going places. If this company keeps growing the way it has been doing, you're going to be a very successful, wealthy man. And I want to be right by your side all the way. I quite fancy being the wife of a rich publishing magnate."

Blake looked as though he'd been punched in the gut. Will's heart went out to him. He tightened his grip around Blake's hand, only to have Blake wrench it free. Melissa saw the movement and smiled cruelly. "Clever boy. *Now* you're thinking sensibly."

Will's heart sank. *Oh God, please tell me he's not even considering it...*

"How long do I have to make a decision?" Blake's voice sounded strangled.

Melissa pretended to consider the question carefully. "Well, it's Christmas in about three weeks' time. And New Year a week later. I always think New Year is such a romantic time to announce an engagement, don't you?" Her eyes glittered. "Well, I'm sure you boys have a lot to discuss, so I'll leave you to it." She beamed, as if all the evil she'd just spewed out was the most natural thing in the world. She walked to the door and turned back to face them. Her face hardened. "Make sure you come to the right decision, Blake." Her eyes met Will's. "Nothing personal, sweet cheeks. Just so long as you know that when I become Mrs. Blake Davis, you'll never get your hands on his dick again. I'm not about to be embarrassed in the media by pictures of you two caught unawares." She tilted her head. "In fact, if I were you? I'd start looking for another job right now. Because once we're married, you're out of here." And with that, she exited the room, leaving Will with the overpowering scent of her perfume and an extremely sour taste in his mouth.

The silence in the room was stifling. Blake stared at the floor, his face ashen. Will ached to comfort him. He waited for Blake to tell him that everything would be all right. When it became clear that no such words would be forthcoming, Will had to say something.

"Blake, if there's anything—"

"I think you'd better go back to your office."

Will stared in dismay. Blake's words were uttered in a monotone, his eyes dull. It was as if a door had closed, hiding the Blake he'd come to care for.

"What?"

"You heard me." Blake's jaw was clenched. Will heard it. He just couldn't believe what he was hearing. "I'm going to spend the rest of the day reading submissions. I don't want to be disturbed." He stared levelly at Will. "Was there anything else?"

Will stiffened. He'd apparently been dismissed. He got to his feet, doing his best to keep his voice even. "No, nothing else." He walked quickly to the adjoining door, not turning once to look back at his boss. There was no way he wanted Blake to see the tears that were welling in his eyes right now. He entered his office and closed the door behind him, leaning back against it. Sorrow filled him.

I feel like I've just lost my best friend. Even as the thought flashed across his mind, Will knew he was lying to himself. *Don't you mean, the man you're falling for?*

Fuck.

CHAPTER EIGHT

"Want to talk about it?"

Lizzie's melodic voice broke through his thoughts. Will looked up from the computer screen he'd been staring at, unseeing, for the last ten minutes to see her standing in his doorway, an expression of concern etched across her face. He gave her a brief smile.

"Not really." Her question didn't surprise him. She was the third person that week to ask him if he wanted to share anything. Rick had been first, of course. Will hadn't felt like sharing a joke with him—well, with anyone—since that hateful day a week ago. And of course they noticed. There were looks, especially during the morning staff meetings. Anyone with half a brain could spot that something was wrong. And if they were worried about Will, heaven knows what must have been going through their minds about Blake...

"Sorry, but I had to ask." Lizzie gave a half smile. "We're all going crazy trying to work out what on earth has happened. Blake is so...."

"Blake has a few things on his mind right now," Will said. "I'm sure it'll sort itself out. Try not to worry." He did his best to make his expression reassuring. Lizzie didn't look entirely convinced, but she shrugged her shoulders and flashed that warm smile once more before leaving him alone.

Will went back to staring at his screen. This week had been awful. Truly awful. Every time he'd been alone with Blake, it had been the same. That sick feeling in the pit of his stomach. Dry mouth. Difficulty swallowing.

Oh, they were talking, but only about work-related issues. No personal conversations. Gone was the warm banter that he looked forward to each morning. He glanced toward Blake's office. The door was shut—literally *and* figuratively.

Will leaned on the desk and put his head in his hands. The Melissa debacle had made one thing crystal clear in his mind—Will had fallen for Blake, hook, line and sinker. Every time he looked at his boss, Will wanted to take him in his arms and hold him close. Blake's tight expression and haunted eyes made Will want to shut out the rest of the world and protect him, keep him safe from anything that would cause him pain. The physical attraction which had been so obvious since the night they met hadn't gone away. Instead, Will felt an emotional connection to the man. Try as he might, he couldn't think badly of Blake. Will could only guess at the torment he was going through. He couldn't blame Blake for reacting the way he had. Trinity Publishing was Blake's life. And when Will weighed up the possible loss of his company, compared to losing a friendship—albeit one with benefits—their relationship must have seemed insignificant in Blake's eyes.

He shook himself. What he really needed was a decent night's sleep. All week he'd tossed and turned, sleeping fitfully, waking hours before the alarm. He only needed to look in the mirror to see the toll it was taking on him. The face that stared back at him could have been Blake's, they both looked so drawn. And Will knew how bad he looked. Even Karen had noticed. Unfortunately, it seemed to have made her more determined to get closer to him, and Will wasn't sure how much more of this he could stand.

His phone warbled. It was a message from Jenny, asking if he could do an escort job tonight. There was an awards ceremony for a marketing company. Will groaned. This whole business was playing havoc with his other job. Even before Melissa had delivered her ultimatum, Will had turned down any clients who wanted sex. He knew he was turning away much needed funds, but he couldn't face the prospect of fucking someone who wasn't Blake. That should have told him how deep his feelings ran. Years of working the streets, having sex with anyone who had the money, had left him able to switch off his emotions. Sure, he could fake it. But along came Blake and bam!—he couldn't even get it up at the thought of having sex with someone else. And since that dreadful day, his heart wasn't in it when he was escorting. More than once a client had rung Jenny to complain about his demeanour. This whole business was killing him.

He glanced at his watch. Time for a coffee. He got up and walked along the corridor to the kitchen. Apparently he wasn't the only one in need of refreshment. Numerous voices spilled out of the room. Was the *whole* team in there? As he entered the kitchen he stifled a groan. Yep. Everyone was standing around drinking coffee and talking among themselves, but all fell quiet as he walked over to the coffee machines. There was an awkward, painful silence. Will poured himself a mug and turned to head back to his office, unable to stand it.

"Will, did you know about our Christmas do?"

Will halted. Sighing internally, he turned to Beth. He tilted his head. "Christmas do?"

Beth nodded. "We're all going out for a meal. We normally do it between Christmas and New Year. The restaurants tend to get booked up fairly heavily before. Would you like to come?" She eyed him anxiously.

"I'd have to check my diary," Will replied, although he knew that if the present situation continued, being sociable would be the last thing on his mind. "Who's 'we'?"

"The team, plus Karen, you... Blake."

Will's chest tightened. "Is Blake going?"

Rick's face was unexpectedly glum. "No one knows. We haven't exactly brought it up with him." Will could understand that. Blake had shut himself off from everyone, not just Will.

"I'll think about it, all right?" Careful nods. Karen entered the kitchen and her eyes widened in surprise. Yeah, it was rare to get so many staff in there at once. She caught sight of Will and her expression changed. Will groaned internally as she sidled up to him and stroked his arm softly.

"How are you doing, Will?" Her voice dripped with honey. "Is there anything I can—"

"Oh, for God's sake, will you just leave me alone?" Will exploded. Startled gasps greeted his words. He was past caring. "I'm going to say this once, loud and clear so you get the message. I. Am. Not. Interested." He gritted out the words, watching as Karen's mouth fell open and her hand flew to her ample chest. "And what's more, I will *never* be interested. For fuck's sake, woman, I'm gay!"

The silence that followed his declaration was so thick, it was almost tangible.

Karen's face was white. She swallowed hard. She flinched as if his words were a physical blow, and then she backed away. The team stood there with equally stunned expressions. A sharp intake of breath had Will turning toward the door. Blake stood there, eyes impossibly wide. Oh fuck. Will held his breath as he waited for Blake to say something, but his heart sank as his boss turned on his heel and walked away.

That was it. Will couldn't take any more. Before anyone could say anything, he put down his mug and fled the room, running to the men's bathroom and locking himself in a stall. He sat on the toilet lid and put his head in his hands. What the fuck had he just done? He stiffened as he heard the bathroom door open and close, listening as feet approached his stall.

"Will? You in there?" It was Rick. *Oh hell.* Will didn't want to talk to him. To anyone. "C'mon, mate, talk to me." There was an edge to his voice, a note of something that sounded like desperation. Intrigued in spite of himself, Will leaned forward and slid the bolt across, slowly pulling open the door. Rick stood there, eyes miserable, looking decidedly jumpy. A look of relief crossed his face when he saw Will. "Oh mate." His voice was unsteady. "When you come out... you *come out*!"

Will couldn't help it. He gave a feeble smile. Rick chuckled.

"You gonna come out here or shall I come in there?" Rick winked. "Wouldn't be the first time I've been in a toilet stall with a guy—if you follow my drift." He locked eyes with Will.

Will barked out a harsh laugh. "I bloody knew it!"

Rick laughed. "Yeah, okay, so I've been thinking the same about you for a while now." Will got up and exited the stall. Rick leaned against the wall as Will ran his hands under the hot tap. All of a sudden they were so cold. "You all right, Will?" The look of genuine concern was touching.

Will expelled his tension in one long push of air as he dried his hands. "Yeah." He'd calmed down a little. Rick was watching him intently. "So... do they know about you?" He flicked his head toward the door.

"Uh-huh. So I'm probably the only person here who was relieved to hear your, er, *declaration*." His eyes sparkled with humour. "Have you any *idea* what's it's been like around here, being the only gay in the village?" They both chuckled at this reference to the comedy *Little Britain*. Rick's expression grew more serious. "So let's try this again. You want to talk about it?"

Will gave him a gentle smile. "Much as I would love to, I can't."

Rick nodded. He stepped toward him, his eyes never leaving Will's face. "Of course, I'd hoped I'd got it right about you." His voice softened. "Do you know how many times I was dying to ask you? The whole situation is so fucking ironic."

Will cocked his head. "What do you mean?"

Rick chortled. "Well, I've been in lust with my boss for six years, for a start." Will's eyes widened. Rick laughed. "Yeah, why are the gorgeous ones always straight? Although now and again, I could've sworn..." He shook his head. "Never mind. Waste of time thinking like that."

He gazed into Will's eyes. "And then *you* turn up, and right from the start you had my gaydar pinging like crazy." He stroked his fingers along Will's arm, Rick's blue eyes never breaking contact with Will's. "I suppose it would be too much to hope that you're unattached." There was a hopeful expression on his face and Will could hear the question Rick was clearly afraid to ask. Oh hell.

"Rick," Will began, his voice gentle, "I'm.... that is...." He sighed. "It's complicated." Rick's face fell and Will felt like a complete bastard. In spite of the way Blake was treating him right now, there was this little part of his brain that hoped they'd work through it somehow. Because Will knew he wanted to be with Blake. He let out a heavy sigh. Yeah, complicated was an understatement. He brought his attention back to Rick. He couldn't lead him on. It wasn't fair. Those soulful eyes regarded him intently. Will leaned forward and kissed his cheek. "I'm flattered. Really. And for the record, you are *very* cute."

Rick flushed, his cheeks a delicate shade of pink. He let out an exaggerated sigh. "Oh well, I had to ask." He touched his cheek briefly and then stepped back. "We still mates?"

"Hell yes." Will grinned. "It's good to know I'll have at least one person in my corner around here."

Rick returned his grin. "Oh, more than one, mate. We like you. Okay, so Karen might have it in for you for a while. She looked bad, I have to say. You hit her pretty hard."

Will nodded, chagrined. He could have done it differently, but it had been a knee jerk reaction. *That's what a lack of sleep and misery will do to you.* "I'll have to apologize."

"Good idea." Rick gestured toward the door. "C'mon, let's get out of here. You'll have them all thinking something's going on in the gents." He winked. "No such luck."

Will laughed and ruffled his tousled hair. "You're a bad boy."

Rick's brows shot up. "You're only discovering this now? *How* long have you worked here?" Both men chuckled and then left the bathroom. The kitchen was empty. Will grabbed another mug of coffee and after giving Rick a warm but brief hug, he went to his office and closed the door. Sitting down behind his desk, he took a drink and gazed at the still closed door. His one consolation was that at least he was out now. Unfortunately it might have made things more awkward for Blake. And judging by Blake's reaction, his boss was distinctly unhappy about this turn of events.

Oh well. It looked as though Melissa was going to get her way after all. Maybe it was time he started looking for another job. It looked as though he was going to need one.

Why the hell wasn't he drunk?

Will couldn't understand it. He sat at a corner table in the club, staring at the empty shot glasses with tired eyes. The music boomed out and the air was filled with chatter. G.A.Y was his favorite club, and tonight it seemed to be the rest of the world's favorite, too. He'd never seen it so packed.

Of course, the go-go boys on stage might have had something to do with it.

He watched them gyrate around their poles, clad only in the skimpiest of silver lycra shorts which showed off their equipment *very* nicely, thank you. Will was hiding. He'd glimpsed a few people he knew, but he was in no mood to talk to anyone. Erroll, his waiter for the evening, sashayed his way past Will's table and gave a quick glance down.

"Another, Will?"

Will hesitated. It was tempting. He'd come out tonight with the express intention of getting drunk, but the alcohol didn't seem to be working. He couldn't understand it. *So a few more shots can't hurt, then.* To his malfunctioning brain, that actually made sense. "Yeah, same again, thanks, Erroll." The boy nodded and waltzed off toward the bar. Will sagged back into the padded seat. Seems like this wasn't his day.

"Where've you been, you bitch? Haven't seen you here in ages!"

Will's head jerked in the direction of the voice. "Oli!" His face broke into a smile.

Oli grinned widely. "Whatcha doin' stuck in the corner, Will? You hidin' from someone?" He winked and Will laughed. "Can I join you?"

"That depends. Where's the wife?"

Oli pursed his lips. "Watch it, bitch. *I'm* the wife." His eyes gleamed. "Ben's at the bar. He'll be here in a sec." Will gestured toward the seat which ran around the table and Oli plonked himself down with a dramatic sigh.

He leaned across and kissed Will exuberantly on the lips before sprawling out across the seat.

"My feet are killin' me. I swear, he's had me on the dance floor for *hours*!"

Will laughed. He knew how much Oli loved to dance, but his passion was fully matched by that of his partner, Ben. The pair could be found at the club most weekends, usually surrounded by a large group of equally gorgeous young men.

"How long have you two been together now?"

Oli's face stretched into a wide smile. "Two years this September." His mouth dropped open. "Ooh! You don't know, do you?" Will was puzzled. Oli held up his left hand and waggled it in front of Will's face. A white gold band adorned his ring finger.

Will grinned. "That's great! When did this happen?"

Oli beamed. "During our trip to New Zealand and Australia." He gave an exaggerated sigh. "It was magical."

"You chatting up strange blokes again, babe?" Ben appeared with their drinks. He winked at Will.

Will loved Ben's Antipodean accent. He was originally from New Zealand but had lived in Sydney for a while before moving to London. He gave Ben a nod as he sat down next to Oli, draping an arm around his shoulder, Oli leaning into him immediately. They made a good-looking pair. Oli was fair and Ben dark, but both men were lean.

Will liked Ben's muscled biceps and ripped torso, his dark blue T-shirt clinging to him. Oli wore his usual jeans and T-shirt, this one depicting two guys embracing. And of course there was the hoodie. Oli and his hoodies rarely parted company.

"Congratulations."

Ben's smile showed off his white teeth. "Aw, thanks, Will." He took a sip of his beer. "We haven't seen much of you around here. You been busy? How's the 'escort' business?" He crooked his fingers into quotation marks and leered.

Will grimaced. "Sore point. I haven't done a lot of work for them recently, to be honest." He glared at Ben. "And I *am* a fucking escort, so watch what you say, bitch!" His grin made it clear he was joking.

"Wait a minute," Oli interjected. "Didn't you have a night of rampant hot sex with a guy? I seem to recall getting a text from you that you were about to have your first client—literally." His forehead creased into a frown. "Did I get that wrong?"

Will sighed. "No, you got it right. And it was only the once."

Ben snickered. "Was it that bad?"

Will chuckled. "Oh, the irony." Both men looked puzzled. "Actually, it was that good. In fact, it was probably the best sex of my life."

Oli's eyes widened. "You're kidding."

Will shook his head. "I wish I was," he said sadly.

Oli gazed at him with concern. "What happened, babe?" Ben's face wore a similar expression. Will was suddenly glad of the opportunity to get the whole mess off his chest. For the next ten minutes or so, he related the story, finishing with the morning's event.

Ben stared at him. "Let me get this straight. You finally told this middle-aged bitch to stop sexually harassing you, and outed yourself in the process?" He guffawed. "Only you, Will."

Oli gave him a dig in the ribs. "Show him a bit of sympathy. Can't you see he's hurting?"

"Ouch!" Ben rubbed his ribs, frowning. "Aren't you being a bit overly dramatic, babe? I mean, it's not like it's going to drastically affect his life there, is it?"

Oli rolled his eyes. "Oh, for a highly intelligent man, you can be so *thick* sometimes." He kissed his partner tenderly on the lips. "Will's in love with his boss," he explained patiently.

Will gave a start. He hadn't said that—had he? Oli was watching him intently, a sympathetic expression on his face. His beautiful eyes grew round as he saw Will's reaction.

"Oh my God," Oli said softly. "And here was me thinking *Ben* was blind."

Will simply stared at him. In love with Blake?

Oli smiled. "Will, the way you look when you talk about Blake, the way you sound... Hate to break it to you, babe, but it's obvious. You're in love with him." He gazed fondly at Will.

Will suddenly felt hollow. "It doesn't matter," he said dully. "He's going to marry Melissa."

Ben snorted. "And you're just going to sit back and let that happen? Like hell!"

"Well, what the fuck should I do? Got any suggestions?" Will demanded. "'Cause from where *I'm* sitting, there isn't a fucking thing I can do about it." His cheeks grew hot.

Ben grinned evilly. "Get him within three feet of me and I'll make him see what a complete ass he's being." His expression changed. He gazed earnestly at Will.

"He's about to make the biggest mistake of his life, Will. Can you imagine the horror his life will be from now on? Married to a total bitch who's not only in it for the money, but also wants him to play it straight. No boyfriends in secret, either. And all because he's afraid to come out."

"Now, hang on," Oli said, laying a hand on Ben's arm. "I can totally see why Blake is doing this. I mean, there's his company at stake." He shifted his attention to Will. "But Ben's right, love. Your Blake is about to ruin his life." There was that sympathetic look again. "If you love him, you can't let him do this—not without telling him how you feel about him."

Will groaned. "Oh hell." They were right, of course. "But what if I tell him and it changes nothing?"

Ben's voice was gentle. "That's a risk you have to take. But think about this: what if telling him changes everything?" He locked eyes with Will.

Will gazed back at Ben. It was a possibility he didn't dare consider. It was too much like tempting Fate. Ben slapped his hand down onto the table.

"Enough thinking. Let's change the subject before you go mad. I've got something else for you to think about. Want to come to Stephen and Darren's place next week?" He leered. "It's gonna be wild."

"Ooh, yeah!" Oli bounced on his seat. "Come with us. It'll be like old times."

Will knew without being told what was taking place at their mutual friends' home. Stephen and Darren were famous for their sex parties. Ben and Oli had actually met at one of their parties just over two years ago.

"The mood I'm in, I'm not sure that's a good idea." Besides, it wasn't something that particularly interested Will. He'd been once, as a guest of Oli and Ben, but group sex wasn't really his thing. He knew the couple played, often sharing a third, but they only played together.

"Aw, please?" Oli shifted along the bench and stroked his hand down Will's chest, before cupping his cheek and kissing him on the lips. "We haven't played with you for ages." His eyes glittered with lust. Will hesitated. He didn't want to offend them, but he wasn't sure he could do that. It felt too much like betrayal.

"It's only cheating if you're actually in a relationship, babe." Damn Ben's intuition. Ben nodded knowingly. "Don't deny that's what you were thinking about. I know you too well." That was true. He and Ben went back longer than he cared to remember, before Oli had come into his life. Ben tilted his head. "Is it something that might interest Blake?"

Now *that* had Will thinking. "Possibly." He remembered Blake all those weeks ago, watching the orgy on his computer. "When is it?" Not that he was going to attend. But it couldn't hurt to know when it was happening. Just in case.

"Next Wednesday." Ben met his gaze. "If by some miracle you *do* get him to come along, you'd better make sure he knows how it works." Oli was nodding next to him.

Will knew what he meant. Anyone who attended a sex party had to know what was expected of them beforehand. He wasn't sure he could go through with it. But if it was something that Blake wanted to do, Will would suck it up and go along. It might be a nice parting gift, their last time together before Melissa got her claws into him. Oli's idea of telling Blake how he felt was romantic, but this was real life, not romance. There was no way Blake was about to give up his company. And it didn't matter if Will was in love with Blake. Blake didn't love him. He couldn't. Because if Blake loved him, he wouldn't be about to give Will up.

Will gazed at the couple. "I'll think about it." That was as far as he was willing to go. Besides, it was a moot point. For him to invite Blake, they'd have to talking to each other, and based on his experience this past week? Wasn't gonna happen.

CHAPTER NINE

I miss him.

For about the umpteenth time that Monday morning, just like every day for the past week, the thought flashed across Blake's mind. He missed Will so much, he ached. And just like every other day, he berated himself constantly. *Why the fuck didn't you stand up to Melissa?* Well, duh. *If you'd told her where to get off, you could be with Will right now.* Blake glanced around his bedroom, remembering Will in his bed, his body curved around Blake's, cock sliding between his cheeks as he fucked him slowly, leisurely.

But it's not just the sex you miss, is it? God, that was so true. Blake missed Will's smile, his sense of humour, the way his eyes lit up when Blake walked into his office. He missed the easy way they used to talk, the way Will anticipated him. He missed the man's efficiency, his confidence. He missed his voice, that rich, deep voice that made him grow warm inside.

Oh fuck. *What have I done?*

What you needed to do.

Blake wasn't so sure anymore. This past week had really brought home how much Will had come to mean to him. With each new day, the pain increased. He watched Will surreptitiously, noting the dark circles under his eyes, the pallor of his cheeks, the careful way he held himself when Blake was there. Will was hurting. And that was Blake's fault.

And it was beginning to dawn on him the magnitude of what he was agreeing to do.

Was the company worth so much to him that he was prepared to be miserable for the rest of his life? He couldn't even comfort himself with the idea of divorcing Melissa after a convenient period of time had passed. Once she got her claws into him, Blake doubted she would be willing to let him go. There would forever be hanging over him the threat of telling his father.

One thing was certain. He couldn't take the cold silence that he'd let build up between them anymore. At first he'd blamed Will. It was all Will's fault. If he hadn't gotten it into his head to fuck Blake in the office, then Melissa would never have caught them out and none of this would be happening. *He'd* started this ball rolling. And then he'd come out to the entire office staff. What the fuck? *All this because I can't be certain if my father is a homophobic asshole.* What if he'd got it wrong? What if Justin Davis turned out to be a perfectly reasonable man who would be delighted to know his son was happy being with a man? Some pretty big ifs there, including the one he didn't dare to voice, as if the mere act of saying it might in some way jinx it. But this was a time for honesty. Fuck it.

What if I'm about to throw away the one man who completes me?

The thought left him weak.

But even if Melissa hadn't come along that day, you wouldn't have done anything to jeopardize your future with the company, would you?

Lying there in the quiet of his bedroom, Blake could be honest. Will had become important to him. But important enough to come out for him?

Well, I'll never know now, will I?

Blake clutched his pillow. If Will was going to be out of his life, he couldn't let him go with this chasm between them, a chasm of his making. So what if he'd blamed Will initially? He didn't blame him anymore. He needed to clear the air, let them part on friendly terms. And the least he could do would be to find him a new position with another company, and give him a glowing reference.

Tomorrow. I'll talk to him tomorrow.

The thought didn't lessen the ache inside him.

Blake pulled open the adjoining door and peered around it. Will sat at his desk, staring at his computer screen, clearly concentrating on whatever he was doing. He hadn't even registered Blake's presence.

"Can we talk?"

Will gave a start, his eyes widening as he caught sight of Blake. "Sorry? Did you say something?"

Blake came into the office and approached Will's desk. "I said, can we talk?"

Will looked startled. Blake couldn't blame him. Blake had been an automaton in their conversations the previous week, keeping things strictly business. "Sure. Here or in your office?" God, the way Will held himself so rigidly. *I did that.* A brief feeling of self-loathing filled him.

"My office. Why don't you grab us both a coffee and then come on through."

Blake couldn't miss the hopeful expression in Will's eyes. "Okay."

Blake gave him a brief smile and then retreated back into his office, trying to ignore the fluttery sensation in the pit of his stomach. When Will came through bearing two mugs of coffee, Blake directed him to the sofa and then sat down next to him. Neither of them spoke for a moment or two, until Blake couldn't take the awkward silence any more.

"Look, first of all, I—"

"Can I just say that—"

Both men regarded each other and then promptly laughed. Will waved a hand. "After you—you're the boss." He spoke lightly enough, but Blake noted the nervous swallowing. He'd run through this conversation so many times in his mind during the night, but now that he was actually here, words failed him momentarily. Will regarded him expectantly.

Blake looked into those warm brown eyes and finally find his courage.

"Will, I'm sorry. I had no right to shut you out the way I have done."

Will stared incredulously at him. "No, you had *every* right! If it hadn't been for me, we'd never—"

Blake silenced his words with a single finger laid gently over his lips. "Let me finish." The words came out much softer than he'd intended. Will became very still, his gaze fixed on Blake. Blake withdrew his hand. "I admit, at first I blamed you. But I have to be honest here. I'm a coward."

Will's eyes grew large, his lips parted. Blake smiled. "No, it's true. I mean, look at me. I'm thirty years old and still in the closet. There are only two people in my life who know I'm gay—I don't count the nameless guys I've fucked—and both those people mean a great deal to me. One is Dave Thurston, my photographer friend." He paused and took a deep breath. "And the other is you." He heard the hitch in Will's breathing.

"Blake," he breathed.

Blake held up his hand. "Still not finished here." His eyes sparkled. "It took this last week to make me realize how much I've come to trust you, respect you, l-like you..." His voice caught on that last part. "I value our friendship too much to let it end like this."

"Is it going to end, then?" Will's face fell.

Blake's heart sank. "I don't see a way around this, babe." The endearment slipped out before he could stop it. He watched it register on Will's face. "I've gone over this so many times in my head. The one stumbling block is not knowing how Dad will react. If I had *any* indication that he'd accept my life, I'd tell Melissa where to get off."

The hopeful light was back in Will's eyes. "Can you be sure he'd react badly? Maybe you've got it wrong. Maybe—"

Blake silenced him once more with his fingers. Will's lips were warm and silky to the touch.

"I can't risk it. This company has been my life for the past six years. I've put so much of myself into it, that I couldn't bear the thought of losing it."

He sighed. "There's still a hope, forlorn thought it may be, that one day he'll look at me and say, 'Blake, I'm so proud of you, of what you've achieved with Trinity. I think it's time to share that achievement with the rest of the world.'" He felt a tear prick the corner of his eye and he wiped it away. *Yeah, some hope.*

Will's eyes had never left him. "I understand, I really do. But if you do this, you're denying a huge part of yourself. You're going to be living a lie."

"Don't you think I *know* that?" Blake's voice rose. "Do you imagine I haven't lain awake all this last week, thinking about how my life is going to be with that *bitch*?" He gave Will a bitter smile. "I can't even console myself by thinking she's doing this because she really wants to be with me. She's in this strictly for the money."

Will huffed. "I whored myself out to survive. What's *her* excuse?"

"Never, *ever* refer to yourself as a whore again in front of me, do you hear?" Blake spoke with quiet vehemence. Will became still. Blake softened. "I mean it." Several seconds passed and then Will nodded.

"So where do we go from here?" he wanted to know.

"I'm going to find you a new job, for starters." Blake locked eyes with him. "You're damn good at what you do, and I'm going to make it my business to find a company that will appreciate you, and help you to further your career. Which leads me on to my next point." He reached into his pocket and withdrew the metallic black USB flash drive. He held it up. "Let me publish this."

Will gaped. "You're serious."

Blake chuckled. "Did you think I was kidding? Hell, no. I want your permission to pass it on to Beth to be edited. You can talk to Peter about any ideas you have for the cover. But I wanted to know—do you want to publish it under your real name or a pseudonym?"

Will smiled. "My real name. No question."

Blake gazed at him with concern. "I only wondered if you might be worried how your parents will react when they—"

"My parents gave up their right to have any say in my life when they threw me out of theirs ten years ago." Will's lips narrowed. "I don't give a fuck if it makes them feel uncomfortable. Let the world see what they did to a fifteen-year-old kid." His lip quavered.

Blake clasped Will's hand tightly. "This is me you're talking to. They're still your parents. You can't forget the first fifteen years of your life just like that." He stroked Will's fingers, gazing down at their joined hands. "Have they ever tried to find you?"

"If they did, they certainly didn't try very hard. As far as I know, we still live in the same city." Blake watched Will's jaw tighten as he straightened. "Anyway, enough of them. About me leaving here. How much notice do I need to give?"

"Don't worry about that. You'll stay here until the right job turns up. That bitch can just put up with it." Blake scowled. "She's getting what *she* wants—she can afford to be a little magnanimous."

"Do I get *my* say now?" Will asked, smirking.

Blake laughed. "By all means."

"Thank you." He gazed earnestly at Blake. "Okay, I agree. You can publish it."

Blake's heart soared. Will snorted. "As if I could stop you anyway." Will paused. "I've loved every minute working here, with you. I've made some good friends, too—well, with the exception of Karen." His face fell slightly.

"Oh, I meant to ask. How has she been with you since your... outburst?"

Will's expression grew gloomy. "I never thought I'd say this, but I actually preferred her when she was flirting outrageously with me.

Nowadays, every time she sees me, she's looking daggers at me. And I can't get a civil word out of her."

Blake whistled. "Be careful there. You know what they say, 'a woman scorned…'"

Will shook his head. "Tell me about it. It's making life very uncomfortable around here. My only consolation is that it seems it won't be for much longer." He swallowed.

Blake felt a pang of guilt. "If there were any other way…"

Will clasped his hand over Blake's. "It's okay, I can cope. Big boy here."

Blake winked. *"Very* big boy."

Will burst out laughing. "Oh, I'm going to miss you." He paused, a blush rising in his cheeks. Blake wondered what was coming. "And in case I never get the chance to tell you… you're phenomenal in bed, Mr. Davis. You rocked my world. Literally."

Blake grinned. "You'll certainly be leaving me with some very vivid memories, that's for sure."

Will's eyes suddenly lit up. "Can we make one last memory together? For old times' sake?"

Blake's eyebrows shot upward. "Why, whatever can you have in mind, Mr. Parkinson?"

Will's cheeks were flushed. "How would you like to experience one of your fantasies?" Blake's expression grew puzzled. "I've been invited to a… a sex party. I wondered if you'd like to attend with me."

Blake caught his breath. "A sex party? I've never been to one. Have you?"

Will nodded. "Once. It was very… educational."

Blake waggled his eyebrows. "I can imagine." He considered the prospect. "Tell me about it. How many people would be there?"

"Three to four couples, max. Or maybe two couples and some singles."

"Do you know them, the people who are hosting the party? And would it be a mixed gathering?"

Will snorted. "Oh hell, no. Strictly gay. And the hosts are a couple of friends, Stephen and Darren. It would be in their home. We're invited by another couple of friends, Ben and Oli."

Blake gazed at him with interest. "*We're* invited? Interesting choice of words. These friends of yours know about me?"

Will's cheeks grew even more heated. "I, er, may have mentioned you."

"Hmmm." Blake was definitely intrigued. "Okay, tell me more. What normally goes on at these shindigs?"

"Actually, if we *are* going to go, I'd have to discuss that with you first." Blake tilted his head. "You have to know what to expect, and more importantly, what would be expected of you."

"Oh, now you have my complete attention." Blake leaned forward, elbows resting on his knees.

"Stephen has built himself a playroom. Some might call it a dungeon."

Blake's cock suddenly decided to take an interest in the conversation. "Oh, really?" He shifted uncomfortably. Will's eyes had a far too knowing expression in them. "Keep talking."

"Well, the only important thing to bear in mind is why you're there. You're going to be having sex with a few people." Will was regarding him carefully. "So you might end up being the meat in someone's sandwich."

Blake recalled his words instantly. Heat flooded through him.

"So..." Will looked at him expectantly. "Is that something you might like to experience?"

Blake opened and closed his mouth, rubbing a hand through his short, black hair. *Oh hell.* On the one hand, he couldn't deny that the idea appealed to him. The number of times he'd watched orgy scenes on DVD or the Internet, and imagined himself in the scene with those sweating, naked bodies, at the mercy of several men. Will really had nailed his fantasy. But on the other hand... Blake's heart stuttered at the thought of watching another man touching Will, kissing him... fucking him. Will fucking someone else. That, he wasn't so sure about. He glanced at Will, who obviously wanted to do this, or else he wouldn't have mentioned it. He was doing this for them. Will seemed to be waiting anxiously for his reply. *I don't want to let him down.* That last thought appeared to be the clincher.

"Okay, let's do it." He smirked. "Talk about going out with a bang." He ignored the tight feeling in his chest that followed his words. At least Will would be there with him. One last night of pleasure before everything changed.

Will gave him a nod. "Okay, I'll let Ben and Oli know we're coming. It's on Wednesday night, by the way." Blake dipped his chin in acknowledgment. "Could we go there in your car? Mine's having a few issues at the moment."

"Yeah, no problem. We can sort out where I pick you up nearer the time." Blake glanced at his watch. "Now, how about you and I do some work?" He winked and Will laughed. Blake heaved a sigh of relief. At least things felt as though they were getting back to normal. But even as he enjoyed that thought, what slipped into his mind next robbed him of all pleasure.

Enjoy it while you can. Before he leaves.

Will stared at his TV screen, his thoughts focused not on the American police series that he routinely watched, but on Blake. He couldn't deny how happy it made him to be on speaking terms again. Yet that happiness was tempered by their imminent parting.

He couldn't bring himself to tell Blake how he felt. Not once Blake made it clear how much Trinity Publishing meant to him. There was no place for Will in Blake's plans, clearly.

What did you expect? A declaration of undying love? Yeah, right. Blake had called it a 'friendship'.

Will had hoped he meant as much to Blake as his boss had come to mean to Will. *Well, at least now I know.* Yes, the sex had been very good, hot even, but apparently for Blake that was as far as it went. And it had been that realization which helped crystallize Will's plans. The party on Wednesday night would be Will's parting gift to Blake, the chance to help his boss live out his fantasy. Will didn't want to think about it. Because each time he did, the thought of watching Blake enjoying another man's touch was too much to bear. So he'd come to a painful decision. Despite Blake's insistence that Will should stay until he found another job, the party would be his farewell. He couldn't stand to see Blake having sex with others, and then see him at work, knowing he couldn't touch him again, kiss him, hold him... Wednesday would be his last day at Trinity Publishing. He'd leave his letter of resignation on Blake's desk for him to find on Thursday morning.

Think how Blake will feel. You're robbing him of the chance to say goodbye.

Will mentally shook himself. He couldn't afford to think like that. He'd just have to make sure their last hours together were memorable. Then it would be a case of finding another job, maybe even moving away from London. He could always do more work for Jenny to keep body and soul together until something more permanent turned up. Even if that meant offering to do more of the personal services that he was presently avoiding like the plague.

Fuck, Blake—you've ruined me for other men. The wry thought should have made him smile. So why did he suddenly feel like crying?

CHAPTER TEN

"Wow." Blake stared in amazement as he swung the car into the long driveway of the large detached house in Harrow, set apart from its neighbours in a quiet, residential area. But then again, *anyone* wanting to live in Harrow had to be made of money.

"Oh yes." Will chuckled. "These two work in the City. They're not short of a bob or two."

Blake pulled up next to a smart new BMW and switched off the engine. He didn't make a move to get out of the car. There were three or four cars parked in front of the house, a mock Tudor house with floodlights which lit up the gravelled parking area. Will sat next to him, watching him with a neutral expression.

It's still not too late, Blake thought. *We could turn around now.* But that wouldn't be fair on Will. "Shall we get in there?" He spoke with more enthusiasm that he actually felt. Will nodded beside him. Slowly they got out of the car and Blake locked it. Before they reached the front door, it opened to reveal a tall, muscular man, possibly in his late forties, with a shock of black hair and pale blue eyes. He grinned when he caught sight of Will.

"I'd given up all hope of seeing you here again, young man."

Will smiled. "Hi, Stephen. Yeah, I've been busy."

Stephen snickered. "Too busy to come and have some fun? My, what a life you must lead." Will introduced Blake and Stephen shook his hand warmly. He gave Blake an appreciative glance. "Hmmm, I know straight away who's going to be monopolizing *you* all night."

He smiled widely and winked. "You're *so* Ben and Oli's type." He looked at Will. "You have excellent taste, boy."

Will gave Blake an apologetic look. "You'll have to forgive Stephen. He finds it *so* difficult to rein in his inner Dom." He grinned at Stephen who beamed.

"Come on in, you two. It's freezing out here." Stephen rubbed his arms vigorously. "Only ten days till Christmas, after all." They stepped into the warm hallway and Stephen closed the heavy, ornate wooden door behind them. He led them toward the rear of the house. Blake could already hear the low, heavily percussive music which pulsed from the room. Once inside, Stephen directed them to several tables in the corner. "You can deposit your clothes there. As you can see, the party's already started."

Blake felt a brief stab of anxiety. This was really going to happen. Then he caught sight of Will's face. Will was regarding him with such a warm look of understanding that it made his heart flutter. *You can do this. Do it for Will.* He gazed around the room with interest. The first thing that struck him was the smell. The air was redolent with the smell of leather and sweat—and something else. He sniffed up carefully. It reminded him of a cross between dirty sweat socks and something vaguely medicinal.

Will smirked and leaned closer. "Poppers, babe." A*ha.* Ben spotted open cabinets piled high with towels, bottles of lube and various diverse toys. There were mirrors strategically placed around the room, and the floor was covered with a thick layer of plastic. A mini fridge stood in the corner.

There was little furniture in the room. What caught his eye immediately was the sling, suspended from a large, sturdy metal frame. What was even more eye-catching was the sling's occupant. A stocky man, his chest a thick mat of hair, lay suspended in it, his feet in stirrups. His head lolled back as another tall man fed him his dick. Blake watched, mesmerized as the guy in the sling swallowed his dick whole: he could see his throat working as his partner thrust deep into him. But the most intriguing thing was what was taking place at the other end of the sling. Another man was slowly pushing a little white ball, which for all the world resembled a tiny snowball, into his anus.

"What is he doing?" Blake whispered, unable to look away. He'd never seen anything like this on his DVDs.

Will brought his mouth to Blake's ear. "You know what Crisco is?" Blake nodded. "Well, they make it up into little balls and wrap them up, then put them in the fridge. It feels great when it's shoved inside you and it's really cold. But then it melts and voila, you're ready to rock 'n' roll." Blake gave a chuckle. Now *that* was ingenious. But the sound died in his throat as he watched the guy encase his dick in a condom and then thrust into his suspended partner. The man in the sling groaned around the thick cock that filled his throat, his groans punctuated by each punishing thrust of the third guy's shaft.

Blake dragged his eyes away from the sight and peered around the room. The lighting was low but enough to make out the varied activities taking place.

In another corner, on a wide seat, a couple were heavily engrossed in kissing and touching each other. They still wore their underwear, but as Blake watched, their hands slid under tight fabric to caress prominent erections which were then pulled free. Any clothing didn't stay on long after that.

Another couple were using a piece of equipment which resembled a picnic table, except that it was padded on the central raised bed with two pads on the lower sections. One guy had his knees there, his belly resting against the upper section. His wrists were shackled to the frame, his arse tilted high as another man ploughed into him, grunting as he went balls-deep, his partner crying out in hoarse pleasure at each thrust. Blake was mesmerized.

All of a sudden he realized Will was tugging at him. "Clothes, Blake. You're wearing far too many clothes." Will's eyes danced with amusement. Embarrassed to be caught ogling, Blake got out of his jeans, sweater and socks, leaving on his briefs. Beside him, Will stripped out of his clothes. With a shock, Blake saw that he'd gone commando. What was more interesting was that Will wasn't hard.

"You okay?" Blake said in a low tone.

Will gazed into his eyes for a moment and then led him by the hand to a free-standing bed, devoid of bedding. He pulled Blake onto the bed and wrapped his arms around him, stroking up his back.

"Been waiting so long to do this again. Kiss me, babe." *Oh God.* That husky voice went straight to Blake's cock which hardened, pushing at the fabric of his briefs.

Their mouths met in a hungry kiss, Blake sinking into it immediately.

God, he'd missed this. Blake caressed Will's body down to where his cock rose up now, thick and hard. *Better.* Will pushed into his hand, hips rocking as their kiss grew more intense.

A slick hand suddenly insinuated itself around Blake's dick. He jumped slightly and broke the kiss with a gasp. Will let out a low noise of disappointment.

"Nice cock, *really* nice." A rich, sexy voice spoke into Blake's ear as that hand continued to tug him, flogging him gently. Blake was shocked into stillness. Will stared beyond him to the owner of the voice.

"Oli," Will moaned softly. Before Blake could react, he was pulled gently onto his back, coming face to face with a nude young man maybe in his mid-twenties, with brown hair. Oli's gaze travelled up and down his body, eyes hooded with lust.

"You must be Blake." Before Blake could utter a word, his mouth was taken in a bruising kiss as Oli explored him greedily. The young man joined him on the bed, stretching out beside him, moving his hands restlessly over Blake's body as his tongue thrust into Blake's mouth, Oli's heavy cock pushing insistently at his hip.

Blake couldn't breathe. It was too sudden, not what he'd anticipated at all. And although it was undoubtedly erotic, Blake was shocked by the thought which slammed through his brain. *But it's not Will. I wanted Will's kiss.*

A second hand stroked up his thigh to wrap firmly around his cock. He stared into dark brown eyes set in a tanned face. *Ben.* Fuck, the man was ripped.

Oli broke the kiss and Blake watched as the couple met over him to kiss passionately, Ben's hand never ceasing in its motion over Blake's cock while he tugged at his own, seven inches of thick flesh which reared up toward his navel, pre-come already showing.

"Oh, you're going to feel *so* good when your arse is tight around my dick," Ben breathed. Blake thought his accent very sexy. "Yeah, me fucking you, while you fuck Oli." Beside him Oli let out a mewl, making it plain he really liked that idea. Blake's heart hammered, his breathing erratic. Something felt wrong, but what, he wasn't sure. He only knew that all of a sudden he didn't want this, knew that with absolute certainty. He started to panic as the two men bracketed him, their heads moving lower until their mouths met at his shaft, two sets of lips sliding over his cock. But by now, far from turning him on, Blake felt dizzy. He was breathing so fast, he thought he was hyperventilating, and his chest felt as if a steel band had been tightened around it.

What the fuck is wrong with me? And then it hit him.

Where the hell was Will?

Will knew how Ben and Oli played. They didn't mess around but simply plunged into the action, working together like a predatory well-oiled machine. The number of times he'd watched them work their magic on some unsuspecting twink at the club, mesmerizing him, working him into a frenzy of lust until he was begging for them to take him home and fuck him. What Will wasn't prepared for was the way it made him feel as they kissed and fondled Blake.

Will couldn't take it. In fact, he couldn't bear it a second longer.

Blake wanted this, remember?

Well, Blake may have wanted it, but Will didn't want to see him get fucked by Ben and Oli—or by anyone else, for that matter. And he wasn't about to stick around and watch it happen.

As Oli moved in position, Will caught sight of Ben, gazing at the couple with gleaming eyes as he moved to join them on the bed. That was it. Will extracted himself from Blake's embrace, Blake too caught up in what Oli was doing to notice, and moved toward the table where he'd left his clothes. He struggled to slip into his jeans, his hands trembled so much, and hastily tugged his sweater over his head. He grabbed his trainers and heavy winter jacket and headed for the door which led into the hallway. As he passed through the doorway, Stephen caught up with him, grabbing him around the arm. His eyes were filled with concern.

"Will, what on earth is wrong? You're as white as a sheet."

Will shook his head. "I'm sorry, Stephen. I can't do this." He glanced back into the room. Blake was hidden from sight by Oli and Ben. "If Blake looks for me, just tell him I left, all right?"

Stephen stared. "*If* he looks for you?" His eyes narrowed. "What's going on, boy?"

Will's leg's suddenly felt weak. The heavy pulse of the music was overwhelming.

"It doesn't matter." His heart was like a leaden weight in his chest. "Sorry, but I've got to go." He shoved his feet roughly into his trainers and slung the jacket around his shoulders. He had to get out of there. Stephen opened the door.

"Are you sure about this? You really want to leave him here?"

Will snorted. "Trust me, Blake can take care of himself. But I think Ben and Oli are doing a pretty good job of that already." One last glance back and then he plunged out into the darkness, his feet loud as they crunched along the gravel drive.

Just get to the railway station, get on a train and go home. That's it, it's over.

Will had never been so miserable in his whole fucking life.

Blake pulled away from the two gorgeous men who looked set on devouring him whole, and gazed around the room in a panic. "Where's Will?" There was no sign of him.

"Chill, babe." Oli gave the room a cursory glance. "Can't see him." He turned back to Blake. "Now, where were we?" He grinned.

Blake couldn't chill. He glanced toward the corner where they'd stowed their clothes and his heart almost stopped. He couldn't see Will's clothes anywhere. He shrugged off Ben's hand on his arm. "There's something wrong."

Ben spoke soothingly. "I'm sure he's around here somewhere." He stroked a warm hand down Blake's back, but Blake shook him off.

"For God's sake, leave me alone. I have to find Will." His heartbeat raced and his mouth dried up. His gaze darted rapidly around the room.

He got off the bed, ignoring the entreaties of the couple to calm down, and ran into the hallway, pulling up his briefs as he did so.

"Whoa, slow down, Blake." Stephen stopped him with a firm hand to his chest. "You need to calm down. You're shaking like a leaf." He led Blake back into the playroom. "Let's get your clothes."

Clothes. Blake's fevered brain latched onto the word and he nodded, following Stephen. He grabbed his clothing and pulled them on, fingers refusing to cooperate. Stephen stood by his side, watching him. Blake picked up his jacket, feeling in his pocket for his car keys. "Got to find Will."

"Blake, he left, about ten minutes ago."

Blake stared at him. There was a painful tightness in his throat. "He *left*? Will wouldn't just leave! Besides, how will he get home? I drove us here!" He ran his fingers through his hair, making it stand up crazily. He had to find Will.

"Then he'll probably be heading for the station. It's a good twenty minutes' walk from here, so if you hurry, you'll catch him up." Stephen clasped his shoulder and squeezed. "Go find the boy."

Blake nodded absently and headed out the front door, the cold night air a shock after the warmth of the house. He climbed into the car and switched the engine on, tires crunching over the gravel as he turned in a tight circle and drove back along the driveway. He scanned the pavements anxiously, peering out into the darkness. *Where the hell are you, Will?*

Suddenly he spied him, shoulders hunched, chin tucked against his chest, walking briskly along the road.

Blake pulled up next to him, braked and rolled down his window.

"Will!" He watched Will jerk his head in surprise as he saw Blake. "What's going on? Please, get in the car."

Will waved a hand at him and didn't slow his steps. "Go back to the party, Blake." His voice was flat. He kept his eyes on the road ahead.

"Please, Will," Blake insisted, keeping an eye on any traffic, "Just get in the car so we can talk about this."

Will's gaze flickered briefly toward him. "What are you doing out here? Go back to the party and have a good time. That's what you came for." That lifeless tone tore at Blake's heart.

"I didn't want to go to the party, all I wanted was to be with you." Will came to a dead stop, eyes fixed on Blake. "Please, Will, just get into the car."

Will stared at him for a moment of two, and then Blake heaved a huge sigh of utter relief as he walked around the front of the car and got in the passenger side. He twisted in the seat to look at Blake, his eyes large and round. Blake noted his cheeks which bore the tracks of recent tears, picked out by the nearby streetlight. For several long seconds, neither of them spoke, the only sound the purring of the engine in neutral.

"We can't sit here all night," Will said at last. "And I think we need to talk."

"Agreed. But before we decide where that conversation will take place, I need to pop by the office. I left my hard drive there and there's stuff on it that I'll need to look over before tomorrow."

"Okay."

Blake drove them through the quiet streets, which grew steadily busier as they neared the city centre.

"I thought it was what you wanted," Will said at last as they drove along.

Blake shook his head. "No, babe. I was only going to the party because I thought *you* really wanted it."

Will let out a shaky laugh. "God, what a right pair we are."

"What a right pair *we* are? Yeah, you're right, we do need to talk."

Blake pulled up in front of the building. "I won't be long, okay?" He got out of the car and dashed up to the main door where he fumbled with the keys.

Will leaned back against the head rest. He still couldn't believe Blake had come after him. His head was buzzing. *What am I going to say to him?*

Well, that would all depend on what Blake had to say, too.

The car door opened and Blake got in. Rather than fastening his seatbelt, he looked at Will keenly for a moment before holding out a familiar looking white envelope.

"Gonna tell me what this is?" He wasn't smiling.

Will's heart skipped a beat. Oh God— the resignation letter. He'd forgotten all about it.

Blake's voice was hard. "You were just going to leave? Without saying goodbye to my face?"

"The party was my farewell gift to you. The chance to live out your fantasy." Will's voice quavered. "I thought it would be easier on both of us if I just walked away, got out of your life."

He bowed his head for a moment. Blake reached for him with trembling hands and cupped his cheek. Will could feel the tremors that rippled through him. Blake tilted Will's head upward.

"Oh, Will." Blake's voice shook with emotion. And then he kissed him.

Will's heart leaped as Blake's lips met his, claiming him in a fierce kiss unlike any other they'd shared. No tongues, just lips pressed together, unwilling to be parted, until Will was dizzy from it. And yet he moved closer, leaning into Blake, seeking more.

How long they kissed, Will had no idea. He only knew he was lost in it. He nuzzled his face into Blake's palm, deepening the contact between them.

At last they parted, their breathing slower, synchronized.

"I only wanted to make you happy," he murmured, fingers combing through Blake's short hair.

Blake gazed at him, a look of puzzlement etched across his face. "Why did you leave me there?"

Will dropped his gaze. "I couldn't watch you be with someone else." He was surprised to hear Blake laugh.

"Oh, babe." Blake smiled. "I felt the same way. When you first mentioned going to the party, all I could think about was having to watch someone else touch you."

Will felt almost giddy. It was more than he could have hoped for. He closed his eyes as Blake moved in for another kiss, this time running his tongue lightly along the seam of Will's lips, the movement sensual. He moaned softly, wanting more, but logic prevailed. Will broke the kiss and leaned back, opening his eyes to gaze at Blake.

"Blake... take me home?"

"Your home?" Will nodded. "Okay."

"And then..." Will hesitated, unsure of giving voice to his thoughts.

"Then?" Blake echoed. He was watching Will, his eyes never leaving him.

"Stay with me tonight?" Will held his breath, waiting.

Blake's face creased into a beautiful smile. "Oh yes. I'd love that."

Will was filled with a lightness of being that seemed to spread throughout his body, filling every part of him.

"Let's go home."

Blake looked around Will's tiny flat. It was on the top floor of a three-storey house and was built into the roof space. Sloping ceilings with large windows set into them gave an impression of cramped space. Blake wondered briefly how Will put up with it, but then he remembered with a guilty pang that Will was trying to pay off his debts. It was probably all he could afford. Heaven knows, rented accommodation in London wasn't cheap.

Will face palmed. "What was I thinking? How can I ask you to stay the night?" Blake tilted his head in confusion. By way of explanation, Will led him by the hand into his bedroom and Blake understood immediately. A single bed stood against the wall, strewn with pillows and cushions.

Blake chuckled. "We're going to be very cozy, that's all." He winked. The flat contained a small living room with a comfy-looking sofa, a rug in shades of red and brown, and a TV, a wet room which consisted of a shower, basin and toilet, and a galley kitchen. His thoughts went to the wet room. "There *is* something I'd like to do, if you don't mind."

Will lifted his eyebrows. "Name it."

"Can I take a shower?" Blake couldn't explain it, but he wanted to wash off any trace of the party. When Will's eyes met his, there was a look in them that told him Will understood exactly what was going through his mind.

"Yes, on one condition." Now it was Blake's turn to arch his eyebrows. Will grinned. "That you share it with me. That's the one room in this place where there's definitely space for two."

Blake could live with that. They undressed in the bedroom, piling the small wicker chair high with clothes, and then Will led him into the wet room. He flipped on the shower and in less than a minute hot water poured out of the shower head.

Will backed into the shower, pulling Blake with him, wrapping his arms around him and kissing him, gently at first, but becoming more sensual as they stood under the deluge, water cascading down, steam puffing out into the room.

Will poured liquid soap into his palms and proceeded to wash Blake, his movements always slow and sensuous. He took Blake's mouth once more in a passionate kiss, Blake gasping as Will slid his hand down Blake's crease to rub over his hole.

Blake moaned and grabbed Will, flipping them until Will's back was pressed up against the wet tiles, water pouring off him and spraying over Blake. He seized Will's wrists and pinned them above his head, Will moaning into his mouth as they kissed, Blake writhing his soapy body against Will, their cocks sliding together in delicious friction. Faster and faster he slid, Will's moans increasing in volume and quantity, until Will was panting breathlessly.

Blake released his wrists and knelt before him, gazing up at Will, his eyelashes beaded with water drops as he slowly took Will into his mouth, licking along his length with a slow, deliberate tongue. He reached up with his hands to caress Will's abs while he moved lower to take his balls into his hot mouth.

"Oh, God, don't stop," Will said weakly.

Blake grinned, his mouth full, and then released them, only to suck Will's rigid shaft into his mouth. Will gave a low cry and thrust his hips forward, propelling his cock deeper. Blake dropped his hands to grab Will's arse, pulling at him, sinking his shaft deeper as he swallowed. Will's hips began to pump, and Blake reached down to pull at his own cock, knowing he was close. He tightened his lips around Will's dick, conscious of the change in Will's breathing.

"Close, babe," Will panted out. "Going to come."

Blake worked his cock faster, exulting in the knowledge that they were going to come together.

Water cascaded off Will's chest, raining down over Blake in a torrent. He slid a finger into Will's crease and pushed the tip into his hole—pushing Will over the edge.

"Oh *fuck*!" Hot come pulsed down his throat, and Blake drank him down eagerly, the smell and the sight of Will in the throes of orgasm giving Blake a final push toward his climax. He moaned around Will's half-hard shaft, his own cock jetting come over his hand, the water washing away all evidence.

Will grabbed him by the arms and hauled him up, claiming his lips in an eager kiss, murmuring into his mouth. They clung to each other, their hands moving slowly over each other's bodies until it felt to Blake that they were memorizing every curve, every muscle, every facet of each other. Their kisses slowed, until at last they parted, Will breathing more evenly, in time with Blake. Will stepped to one side to grab two large towels, and handed one to Blake, but rather than dry themselves, they elected to dry each other with care, rubbing hair until it was merely damp.

"Come to bed."

Blake nodded eagerly. Will led him into the bedroom and drew back the covers, getting in first and pressing his back up against the wall. Blake climbed in and pulled the sheets over them both, before dragging Will into the centre of the bed.

"You're not sleeping cramped up like that. I want you in my arms tonight." Will caught his breath, his eyes shining. Blake took Will in his arms, hooking his leg over Will's hip, anchoring them together.

"We can't fall asleep like this," Will protested weakly.

Blake leaned close to murmur into his ear. "But think of the fun we'll have trying." Will chuckled.

Blake stretched back and switched off the lamp, throwing the room into semi darkness. The glow of streetlights could still be seen through the windows. He tightened his arms around Will. It felt so right, lying like this.

How can you even think of giving this up?

The answer to that was easy. He couldn't, not now.

The hard part would be to work out how to keep him.

CHAPTER ELEVEN

"What are you doing tomorrow night?" Dave slipped in the question at the end of their weekly catch-up chat.

Blake leaned back into his chair and thought hard. "Wednesday. Nothing at the moment. Except wrapping presents for this lot." Thursday was Christmas Eve and although the office would be open, it was only a half day. Traditionally there was a final team meeting, followed by a small party where the team exchanged gifts, nothing too extravagant. Everyone drew a name in secret and could only spend a maximum of twenty pounds on that person's gift. Blake had drawn Karen this year, and her present was causing him some concern. Lately she was snapping at everyone, Will in particular. Rick had hinted there might be troubles at home with her boyfriend, a bricklayer who reportedly kept Karen on a short leash.

Blake's gift to Will was already sorted. He'd got together with Beth and given her Will's book, asking for her discretion once she'd read it. She'd carried out the edits in one night, and had passed it back to him the following day, her eyes shining. She'd clearly found it as moving an experience as Blake had. Strictly speaking, it should have gone to Will to accept or reject the edits, but Blake had a plan. He'd had run up a one-off copy, together with a cover designed by Peter. He wanted to give Will a taste of how it would be to have his own book in his hands. After New Year, they'd go through the whole process properly, but Blake wanted to surprise him.

"How would you like to come to dinner tomorrow night? My treat."

Blake whistled. "Oh wow. Better write this one in the diary." He grinned, waiting for Dave to react. He didn't wait long.

"You cheeky sod. I paid last time, if you remember."

Blake chuckled. "Yeah, I do, actually, so you must be after something. Out with it."

"Well..." Dave hesitated. "The offer is for both you and Will." Blake was stunned. He'd taken Dave out for a pint last Thursday night and told him about Melissa's ultimatum. Dave's reaction had been almost explosive. He demanded to know why Blake would even contemplate giving in to her demands. Then his mood changed. He'd asked quietly how Blake felt about Will.

Now there was a question.

Blake could no longer deny he had feelings for his PA. And the depth of those feelings continued to surprise him. As New Year came closer, the thought of giving up Will filled him with sorrow. He wasn't sure he could do it. Not now. It had only been a week since the party, but already the difference in their relationship was apparent. The most noticeable thing was that Will had spent every night in Blake's bed. In fact, in the last few days, he'd taken to leaving a change of clothes at Blake's apartment so he didn't have to crawl out of bed at stupid o'clock in order to go home and get ready for work. Blake had to admit he liked it. At work he knew he was walking around with a huge grin on his face, but he didn't give a damn. And of course, everyone noticed. He could see his team dying to ask what had turned him into Mr. Happy all of a sudden, but typical of them, no one had broached the subject, not even Ed.

And as long as neither Blake nor Will mentioned Melissa, Blake could ignore the elephant in the room for a little longer.

Dave had been delighted to learn about Will. And as for asking them both to dinner, it would be their first outing as a couple.

A couple. Why are you deluding yourself like this? You know *it can't go anywhere.*

Yeah, Blake knew. They both did. Oh, it had been a blissful week—that much was true. Long nights together, lying in each other's arms, enjoying each other's bodies. Waking up each morning to see Will beside him, curled up in his arms. Putting up a Christmas tree and decorating it together. But yes, they were deluding themselves. They tried to pretend it was bliss. Tried to make it anything other than what it was—their final moments together. Ticking away, one by one. The two men snatched bits of time wherever they could. Furtive kisses in Blake's office when they were sure no one was around. Eating together. Every glance was memorized, every touch cherished. Every kiss filed away to keep them warm on the lonely nights that lay ahead.

Blake snapped out of his internal wanderings. "Dave, I think that's a lovely idea. Eating out or your place?" Dave had an apartment above his studio.

"My place. And I'll order in. You know what my cooking is like."

Blake snorted. He and Dave had shared accommodation at university, and he still had vivid memories of Dave's first cookery 'experiments'.

"Ooh, now you've *definitely* sold me. I'll be sure to bring the Gaviscon tablets. Just in case." He chuckled as Dave gave out a low growl. "What time?"

"Seven? Think you two can manage to tear yourselves away from that hive of industry you slave away in?"

Blake chortled. "Yeah, I think we can manage that. This assumes, of course, that Will says yes."

"Do your best. I need to see you both."

Now Blake was *really* intrigued.

"Mind if I use your bathroom?" Will asked.

"It's along the corridor on the right," Dave directed him. "I'll have coffee ready by the time you come back." Will smiled warmly as he exited the kitchen. Dave sidled over to where Blake was stuffing the Chinese takeout boxes into the trash. "I like him, Blake," Dave said quietly. "Seriously. He's intelligent, thoughtful, and sexy as hell, even to a straight like me." He locked eyes with Blake. "You can't let this guy get away."

Blake groaned softly. "That's right, rub it in."

Dave placed his hand on Blake's arm. "I'm sorry. I didn't think." He stared at the door where Will had stood seconds earlier.

"Er, Dave? Coffee?" Blake's voice was tinged with amusement.

Dave visibly shook himself. "Sorry. It's just I've never seen you so damn happy." He let out a growl. "That bitch. Just don't invite me to the wedding. I'll strangle the cow."

He went to the worktop and began dumping coffee into the paper filter, making small discontented noises. Blake would have been amused but he was too busy trying to push down the feelings which rose to the surface on hearing Dave's words. Letting Will go was the last thing he wanted to do. But Dave mentioning the wedding brought the reality of the situation home to him in a cold rush of fear. How much longer did he have Will to himself? Not long enough.

"I can't smell the coffee yet." Will was standing in the doorway, arms folded. "You two have been gassing, haven't you?" His eyes twinkled. He turned to Dave. "Thank you, by the way, for the invitation. It's been great to meet you. And I love your work." Dave gave him a puzzled look. "Your prints? In Blake's apartment?"

Dave's brow cleared, and then his cheeks flushed. "Funnily enough, I was thinking about those prints only recently."

Blake eyed Dave speculatively. "Aha, *now* we're getting to the point of the invitation. Come on. I knew you had an ulterior motive." He winked at Will.

Dave looked decidedly guilty. "Let's go and sit down in the lounge with our coffee, and I'll come clean." Will's eyebrows lifted and he gave Blake a questioning glance. Blake shrugged, picked up his coffee mug, and followed Dave out of the kitchen. The three men took their seats, Dave in an armchair and Blake and Will on the sofa. Blake liked the fact that Will leaned into him immediately. It was nice to sit there and feel the warmth radiating from his body. He draped an arm around him and pulled him closer. *God, this feels good.*

Dave studied his coffee mug for a few seconds and then looked at Will.

"Just so you know, I do mostly portrait work—graduation photos, family shots, weddings—although I have to be honest, the wedding side of things has dried up a little lately. Not really surprising." He took a long drink of his coffee, his expression gloomy. "In these recession-hit times, the happy couple are more likely to fork out for the dress and the reception, but get a talented friend to take their pictures instead of hiring a photographer."

"Yeah, I can understand that," Will said, giving Dave a sympathetic look.

"So, I decided to drum up some business by branching out into a new market." Dave cleared his throat. "I, er, took out an ad in GT and Attitude magazines."

Will whistled. "Gay Times mag? Attitude? Not going to ask how much *that* set you back." He pulled a face. Blake was impressed with Dave's initiative.

Dave shrugged. "It was a one-off. I thought I'd see if anything came of it. If it was a waste of time, I wouldn't do it again. But with more and more gay couples getting married—sorry, entering *civil partnerships*—I figured there had to be some business there. And if a client wanted something more... intimate, I could do that, too." He indicated Blake with a flick of his head. "I mean, just look at the ones I took of *him*. If I could cope with those, I can cope with anything." He chuckled.

Will's eyes gleamed appreciatively.

"Dave, they're beautiful. But I have to ask you something. However did you get him to agree to doing them in the first place? And get him to jerk off for you on camera?" His hand snuck across to stroke leisurely across Blake's belly, and Blake could have purred with pleasure.

Dave guffawed. "I can tell you that in one word—tequila! And as for getting His Majesty over there relaxed enough, I pulled up some gay porn on my laptop. Didn't take long for *that* to work." He stared hard at Blake. "And let's not forget here exactly *whose* idea that shot was."

Blake's cheeks were red hot. "Okay, enough of that." He gave Dave a meaningful stare. "I'm assuming something came of your ad, or you wouldn't be sharing with us now."

Dave straightened. "You'd be correct. A month went by and I heard nothing, so I was about to write it off as an expensive whim, when I got a phone call. A guy wanted a set of prints doing for his apartment and he requested to see my portfolio. So he came to the studio, and after some humming and hawing, I finally got it out of him that he wanted some intimate portraits, definitely sensual, but I could veer toward erotic if the mood took me. I showed him your prints, Blake, and he loved them."

"Hardly surprising—they're beautiful," Blake said loyally.

"Which brings me to the point of your being here." Dave put down his mug on the coffee table and faced them. "I want you to pose for me. Both of you." Blake opened his mouth immediately to protest but Dave plunged ahead. "Just like before—no head shots—simply the two of you being yourselves in an intimate setting."

Will tilted his head. "*What* setting?" He was clearly intrigued.

Dave grinned and crooked his finger, "Come with me." Will unfolded himself from the sofa and extended a hand to Blake. Dave led them out of the living room and down the stairs into the photography studio. Blake had been there many times, once as an observer while Dave had been working. He glanced at Dave's main work area. The large white backdrop was already set up, but in front of it on the floor were piles of white pillows and a white sheet. The lights were on and there were steps placed around the makeshift bed, obviously for when Dave wanted to take shots from a higher angle. Dave's camera was on his work table, along with his filters and lenses.

Will stared. "Oh wow." He turned to Blake, eyes shining. "I want to do this." He was almost vibrating with excitement. There was no way Blake would disappoint him when he was clearly so eager. Dave was watching the pair of them, a hopeful expression on his face.

"Okay," Blake said at last. "Let's do this." Dave's woot of joy made him chuckle. "How do you want us?"

Dave leered. "Nude—and under that sheet." Then his face cleared and he blushed. "There's a screen over there if you're shy about undressing in front of me." Blake knew he was addressing Will.

Will snorted. "Yeah, right, like *that's* gonna be an issue." He grinned at Blake and waggled his eyebrows. "Let's get naked, babe."

Blake laughed as Will grabbed the hem of Blake's sweater and began to pull it up roughly, his face creased into a joyful smile.

Will's mood was infectious. Blake got in on the act and the two men stripped each other, laughing and giggling, especially when Will tried to tickle Blake's ribs. Blake's peripheral vision caught Dave already clicking away quietly with his digital SLR camera, but Blake shut him out and concentrated on his lover. Nude, they fell onto the pillows, laughing. Will pulled the sheet up over their heads and reached for him, taking his mouth in an eager kiss, Blake responding immediately.

"Hey! Not fair! Get out from under there, you two!" Dave's amused exclamation made Blake laugh.

Will chuckled but then pushed the sheet down, revealing their upper bodies. He pulled a face at Dave. "You're no fun."

Dave shook his head. "I might have known you'd be trouble. Okay, you two—pretend I'm not here. I'm just going to take as many shots as I can, either from down here or up there." He indicated the steps with a wave of his camera. "I'm not going to direct you, unless I see something that would look really good. Talk to each other, touch each other. Just be yourselves."

Blake could do that.

He pulled Will to him and kissed him, winding his arms around Will's body and holding him close. Then he lost all track of time. They laughed quietly, rolling around on the pillows. They lay next to each other, hands reaching for each other, caressing each other. Now and again Dave issued a quietly worded request, but for the most part Blake was unaware of his friend's presence.

It was a magical feeling, as if time had somehow been suspended, trapping them in this bubble where only the two of them existed. No Melissa. No farewells on the horizon. Just him and Will.

It was a shock when Dave's voice pierced through the quiet euphoria.

"Okay, guys, that's it."

Blake stared in surprise. "Already?" He didn't want to move. And then Will looked at him with an expression which told Blake in no uncertain terms that this wasn't over, merely postponed until he got Blake into bed. Will smiled. Yeah, he could tell Blake had gotten the message. Blake's cock certainly had. He was so hard, he ached.

"Already?" Dave echoed. "I've been taking shots for the last hour." He chuckled. "You were obviously enjoying yourselves too much." He grabbed his camera and memory cards. "You two get dressed and I'll meet you upstairs. I want to load these onto my laptop right away." He left them to it and headed for the stairs.

Will kissed Blake, running his hands down Blake's spine to cup his arse, pulling Blake against him so that he could feel Will's prominent erection against his own. "You and me. Tonight. Making love. For hours." His voice was husky.

Blake caught his breath. It was the first time Will had used those words to describe their coupling. "I like the sound of that." He pushed at Will's lips with his tongue, and Will responded eagerly, giving him entrance. They kissed passionately for several minutes, until Will pushed him away with a loud groan.

"This isn't good. We're never gonna get dressed at this rate."

Blake chortled. "You take your time. I'll get dressed and go on up there so he doesn't think we're up to something." He arched his eyebrows. "Tempting though that thought is, right now."

Will laughed. "Later. Promise."

Blake's laugh echoed his. He pulled on his clothes, and carrying his trainers and socks, headed up the stairs to Dave's apartment. He found Dave sitting at his dining table, staring intently at his laptop screen. Dave looked deep in thought. As Blake approached him, he looked up, startled.

"Sorry, I was miles away. I was just checking out some photos I took of this couple."

"What was so engrossing?" Something in Dave's expression piqued Blake's interest.

Dave let out a sigh. "Sometimes—not often, I'll admit, but once in a while—I take a photo that blows me away by how much it reveals. The camera captures more than I'd intended." He glanced down at the screen. "This is such a photo. I look at these two people and when I see the emotion I've caught in one brief click... Wow."

"Can I see it?" Blake couldn't contain his curiosity.

Dave smiled. "Sure." He turned the laptop to face Blake—and waited.

Blake was shocked into stillness. It was him and Will, both lying on their backs, Will's head resting on Blake's shoulder. Will was craning his neck to stare up at Blake. What made the breath catch in his throat was the expression in Will's eyes. Love shone out of them. It was unmistakable.

"You see it, don't you." Dave's quiet statement crept out into the silence which had ensued.

Blake nodded, unable to tear his eyes away from the screen. Then he studied his own image and his throat tightened. The expression in his eyes could have been the mirror image of Will's.

"I want this photo," Blake whispered. He was dimly aware of Dave nodding. Finally he broke free of the photo's spell. "Can you do me a print, just like the others?"

"Sure." Dave shoved a USB flash drive into one of the ports and clicked on the photo. He took out the flash drive and handed it to Blake. "But in the meantime, here's a copy of it."

Blake took it absently, his eyes drawn back to the screen. The sound of Will approaching had him looking away hastily. Dave caught his mood and snapped down the laptop, just as Will entered the room. Blake gave Will a relaxed smile, trying to ignore his racing heartbeat. "It's getting late. How about you and I head home?" The word stuck in his throat. Home.

Will nodded. "Did the photos turn out all right?" he asked Dave.

"Just beautiful. I'll let you see when I've cut off your heads—if you get my meaning." Dave smirked. He glanced at his watch. "And now you two need to get out of here. It's already past my bedtime."

Blake rolled his eyes. "I see how it is. Now you've got what you wanted, you're casting us off like an old shoe." He loved teasing Dave.

"Yep." Dave folded his arms and grinned. "But thanks for that. You two are very photogenic." He held out his hand to Will. "It was a real pleasure to meet you, Will."

Will shook his hand. "Same here." He turned to Blake. "Okay, you, take me home."

Blake speared him with a look. "On one condition." Will's eyebrows lifted. "That you don't grope me again as we go through my building. Dominic's the doorman on tonight, and the last time he was on late night duty, you kept touching my arse as we walked to the elevator. He didn't know where to look."

Will guffawed, but then straightened his face and made a cross over his heart. "I'll be a good boy. Promise." He pressed his lips together in what he obviously hoped was an innocent expression. *Yeah, right...*

Blake hugged Dave tightly and then took hold of Will's hand.

"Let's go home."

He had an appointment with a bed, his lover—and if he was really lucky, Will's leather wrist shackles.

CHAPTER TWELVE

"I really like this idea," Will confided in Rick as he glanced around the conference room. Christmas songs were playing in the background, and the table was loaded down with brightly wrapped gifts, plates of party food and bottles of wine and soft drinks. Once the meeting had taken place that morning, Rick and Lizzie had shooed everyone out of the room to set up the party. Not that any actual *work* got done by anyone. Lots of coffee drinking in the kitchen and standing around chatting, yes. It was Christmas Eve, after all. The only puzzling part had been Karen's non-appearance. She hadn't rung in sick, but as yet there was no sign of her.

"Yeah, the boss has done this every Christmas Eve since he took over." Rick's face fell. "Took over. Yeah, *right*."

"What's the deal there?" Will asked. It was something he'd been meaning to broach with Blake, but it was clearly a sore point. "Does Blake own the company or Justin?"

Rick sighed. "When the old man had his heart attack, Blake stepped in at his request. Justin said at the time that he was giving Blake the company, and that Blake was to run it as he saw fit. So out with the old, in with the new."

"So it *is* Blake's company."

Rick snorted. "Except Justin hasn't let go. No public announcement of Blake's takeover of command, no acknowledgment of Blake's achievements. Hell, Justin is still taking the credit for all Blake's success."

He scowled. "That must *really* piss off the boss, especially when Justin wanders in and keeps sticking his oar in all the time." He puffed out his breath.

"Is the company legally Blake's?"

Rick met his gaze. "Good question. I don't know, is the answer to that one." He glanced at his watch. "Hey, it's almost twelve. Why don't you go grab the boss and drag him out of that office so he can come play with the rest of us kiddies?" He grinned and then his expression grew more sober. "I'll try ringing Karen again. This isn't like her."

"Good idea." Will thought Rick was a really sweet guy. He clearly cared a lot for his workmates. Will left him and went along to Blake's office. Blake was perched on the arm of the sofa, staring down into the street far below. There was a faraway look in his eyes that Will recognized immediately. He'd seen a lot of that look in the past week.

He pushed the door shut and then walked over to Blake and laid a hand on his shoulder. "The troops are ready for inspection, Sir," he said with a wink.

Blake turned slowly toward him, his face upturned. "Kiss me."

Will was momentarily taken aback. He hadn't expected such an opening, but hey, he would never turn down a request like that. He lowered his head and brought his lips to meet Blake's, the kiss tender and lingering. Blake closed his eyes, sighing, the sound lost as Will deepened the kiss.

When he broke away to gaze down at Blake there was something in Blake's expression that caused Will's heart to give a jolt.

"What's wrong, babe?"

Blake opened his mouth to speak, but then a sudden commotion coming from the conference room halted him in his tracks. He frowned. "What's going on out there?" Will tilted his head, listening. Something was obviously wrong. Blake got to his feet and walked purposefully to the door, Will close behind him. When they entered the conference room, both men gasped. Karen was standing by the table with a couple of uniformed police officers. A female police officer held Karen's arm, clearly trying to calm her. The team was standing around, everyone wearing similar expressions of shock and concern. What drew Will's gasp, however, was Karen's face. Her left eye was blackened and puffy, her cheekbones bruised and swollen and there was a nasty looking cut to her top lip.

"My God, Karen, what happened to you?" Blake approached her, his face contorted in distress. Karen ignored him and turned toward Will, her face suddenly a mask of panicked fear. She pointed a trembling finger at him.

"That's him. That's the one." The police officers turned toward Will. The male officer pulled out his notepad and more worryingly, a pair of handcuffs. *What the fuck?*

"What's going on here, officer?" Blake took charge, his voice cool and calm. "I'm Blake Davis, the CEO of Trinity Publishing."

The officer acknowledged Blake with a polite nod. "Ms Candido here has reported that she was assaulted last night. She called the station to report this about an hour ago, and asked us to meet her here. Ms Candido claims that the assault was carried out by your PA, Will Parkinson."

His eyes alighted on Will. "That would be you, sir?"

Will stared in absolute horror, his mouth open. No words came out. Cold spread throughout his body at the thought that Karen could do something so vile. Then sanity was restored. It didn't matter what she said, there would be no physical evidence. Whoever had bashed her face would have to have some tell-tale signs, such as bruised knuckles. It still didn't detract from the fact that she was accusing him, in front of everyone. He stiffened as the officer approached him.

"Will Parkinson, you are under arrest for the assault of—"

"What the hell is going on in here?"

Justin Davis stood in the doorway, his face flushed. Will stifled a groan. Talk about bad timing. A swift glance at Blake sent his heart sinking. Blake had paled.

"It's okay, Dad, I'm dealing with this." Blake turned to the male officer. "I think there's a mistake here, officer." He rubbed at the back of his neck, blinking rapidly.

Will held up his hand to silence him. "Blake, it's okay. You just get on with the party. I'll go down to the station and we can clear this mess up there." Will met Blake's gaze. "I'll be all right." Blake's mouth twisted into a grimace. Will turned to the male officer. "Let's get on with it, shall we?" The officer nodded, opening his mouth to continue with his warning.

"He's innocent. You're making a grave mistake."

Blake's outburst rang out loudly in the quietened room. Will stared fixedly at him. "Leave it, Blake." He tried to convey with his eyes that it really was okay.

Blake addressed himself to the officer. "Will didn't do this. He couldn't have." Blake's eyes flicked briefly to Will. "He was with me all last night." *Oh my God....* Will's heart almost skipped a beat. He could hear the sharp intake of breath from several people around the room.

Justin blanched. "What are you saying, Blake?" He was staring very hard at Blake.

Blake ignored his father and reached into his pocket. "I don't expect you to take my word for it," he said to the officer. "There's a photo on this flash drive that was taken last night, and I'm sure it will be time stamped. You'll see both of us on it. I will also give you the contact details for the friend who took the photos. And finally, you can contact the night doorman of my apartment building, who'll confirm that Will arrived with me last night, not long after the photo was taken, and that he didn't leave until seven this morning when he left with me to come here. So there is no way that Will was anywhere near Karen last night." Blake finally turned to face Will, his eyes shining. "He was with me." The repeated words were uttered quietly.

Will stared at him in stunned silence, overwhelmed by the magnitude of what Blake had just done—for him. "Why, Blake?"

Blake walked toward him and took his hand. He looked into Will's eyes, his expression calm. "Because I love you."

The gasps which followed his words were louder this time. Will's jaw dropped. *Blake loves me.* Not only that—Blake had just declared his love in front of an audience which included his father.

Warmth radiated throughout his entire body, and he was conscious of his heart pounding strongly. A grin spread across his face. He couldn't tear his eyes away from Blake's beautiful face, where a similar grin matched his own. "You love me."

Blake's eyes danced with joy. "Yes." That one word sent Will's heart soaring even higher. Then a faint crease appeared between Blake's eyes. He swallowed. "Do you love me?"

Will wanted to take him in his arms there and then and kiss away the doubt that was clearly etched across his face. "Oh God, yes." He locked eyes with Blake. "I love you, too."

Blake opened his mouth to speak, but whatever words he'd been about to utter were lost in a loud wail from Karen. She collapsed into the arms of the WPC, sobbing wholeheartedly. Despite his revulsion at what she'd attempted to do, Will crossed the room to stand in front of her, his mind still whirling at Blake's declaration.

"Why, Karen? Why would you do this? And more importantly, who did this to you?" Karen wouldn't meet his gaze. "Come on, Karen, tell us." She shook her head stubbornly.

"I think, sir, that those are questions which should best be asked down at the police station," the male officer stated in an undertone. "There's a little pressing matter of wasting police time to be addressed, for a start." He gave a nod to his partner, who started to guide Karen out of the office. "My apologies, Mr. Parkinson." Will bobbed his head briefly. They escorted the weeping Karen from the building. Will hoped they got to the bottom of it. Because *someone* had certainly taken out their rage on Karen's face.

"Don't you think you owe me an explanation?"

Will saw Blake's jaw tighten as Justin marched up to his son, his face still pale. Blake drew himself up to his full height and faced him.

"Actually, Dad, my private life has nothing to do with you."

Justin's eyes blazed. "It is when it affects my company. I—"

"And there we have it. *Your* company." Blake scowled. "Whatever happened to 'it's your company, son'? 'Put your stamp on it.' Does any of this ring a bell?" Justin's gaze lowered and Blake jutted out his chin. "Well, I did all that, Dad, and more. So please, tell me how me being gay is going to affect the company for one second."

There was a long silence as the two men faced each other. Will was aware of the whole team watching the spectacle. He walked to Blake's side and slipped his hand around Blake's. Blake gave him a quick grateful glance. Justin said nothing, his throat working as he swallowed. Will held his breath, waiting for Justin's reaction. When it became clear he wasn't about to say anything, Blake's hand tightened around his.

"You know what? I've had it." Blake snapped out the words. "If you're not prepared to acknowledge everything I've done during the last six years, then I'm out of here. You can *keep* your precious company." Will gaped.

"You're not serious." Justin's eyes goggled.

"Watch me." Blake stared resolutely at him.

Justin's jaw dropped. "But...but what will you do?"

Blake barked out a laugh. "That's easy. I'll start up my own publishing company."

"And where the boss goes, we go." Ed came to stand beside Blake, flinging his arm around his shoulder. "Right, guys?" There were murmurs as Blake's team moved as one to stand behind him, all eyes on Justin. Will was so proud of them for this show of solidarity. He glanced at his lover and was dismayed to see him tremble.

"Is that what you really want, Dad?" Blake's voice softened. "Are you prepared to lose everything this company has gained, just because you're ashamed to have a gay son?"

Justin's eyes widened in alarm. "Wait... you think I'm ashamed of you?"

"Well, what else am I supposed to think?" The misery in Blake's expression tore at Will's heart.

Justin shook his head. "Forgive me, Blake. For my generation, being gay was something you didn't shout about. I know it's all different these days, but I guess I'm still stuck in the past. I'll be honest, my first reaction was to wonder how the company would be perceived if it became known that its owner was gay."

Blake snorted. "No one will bat an eye, I promise you." He became still. "You... you don't mind that I'm gay?" Will saw the hopeful light in Blake's eyes and held his breath, praying for Justin's reaction.

"Of course I don't mind." Justin fixed his gaze on his son. "All right, so it's something I didn't expect, but it doesn't change how I feel about you." He tilted his head. "Why would you think you being gay would bother me?"

Blake's mouth fell open. "But... but what about Uncle Dominic?"

Justin frowned. "I don't understand. What does your uncle have to do with any of this?"

Blake stared in amazement. "I remember how you were whenever he came round to see me. You couldn't stand to be in the same room as him."

Justin burst into laughter. "Oh, Blake." He shook his head, smiling sadly. "I couldn't stand to be near him, you're right, not because he was gay, but because he was an obnoxious son of a bitch!"

Blake's expression was incredulous. "What?"

Justin scowled. "That bastard was always asking for money. He drank like a fish and was forever running up bad debts. He owed money to nearly every betting shop in London at one point." He stared with wide eyes to see Blake's face. "You really thought I didn't like gays?" When Blake nodded numbly, Justin's face fell. "That tells me how much we've grown apart—and that saddens me immensely."

Blake blinked. "But... what about your reaction to Trinity publishing gay fiction? I thought you were against it?"

Justin sighed. "No, that wasn't it. I was just nervous that it wouldn't pay off. And then we're back to the whole 'older generation' bit again."

He locked eyes with his son. "You were right, of course. The genre is growing ever more popular. It was the right decision—only one is a long line of good decisions, I have to say."

He moved closer to Blake and Ed stepped back, allowing him access. Justin grasped Blake's shoulder firmly. "I'm proud of you, son."

The look of joy in Blake's eyes was almost too much to bear. Will fought hard to hold back tears. "Dad?"

Justin became still. "Yes, son. I should have said this a long time ago. And I think I clung on to the company when I should have made a clean break of it." He placed his hands on Blake's shoulders and regarded him squarely. "But we can do something about that."

Will hardly dared breathe as he saw the hopeful expression on Blake's face.

Justin smiled. "I think it's time we made this official, don't you? I'll prepare a press statement for tomorrow, to the effect that you are the legal owner of Trinity Publishing, and have been solely in charge of the company for the last six years. Think of it as your Christmas present." He winked, but then his expression changed. "I'm sorry to have spoken so disparagingly of your team, Blake. The way they all rallied round you was truly wonderful. You chose a fine bunch of people, son." He fixed the team with a forthright stare. "And I believe you're supposed to be having a party here, so why don't you good people get it started while I take my son and his...partner into his office for a talk?" He winked. "We won't be long—wouldn't want to miss you opening your gifts!"

There were smiles all round as Justin led Blake and Will to Blake's office and then closed the door behind them.

Blake seemed to be in a dream. He kept staring at his father openmouthed, blinking. Justin regarded him with a hint of anxiety in his expression.

"Are you all right, son?"

Will reached out and squeezed Blake's hand tightly. Blake gave him a grateful glance before meeting his father's gaze. "Yes, Dad, I'm fine."

Justin gazed back at him for a moment and then held out his hand to Will. "I'm pleased to meet you, Will. I hope to get to know you better."

"I look forward to that too, sir." Will shook his hand.

Justin chuckled. "Sir seems a little too formal for the present situation. Justin will do fine." He tilted his head. "So, I have to ask... does Melissa know?" His eyes twinkled.

Blake shuddered. "God, no." He paled. "Hell, you don't know what's been going on." Swiftly he related the events of the last few weeks. Justin's face became a mottled shade of purple.

"That little conniving bitch." He spat out the words. "Wait till I see Bill." Bill Richards was Melissa's father and one of Justin's closest friends. "He'll disinherit her. That'll hit her where it *really* hurts."

"Wait, Dad."

Will looked at his lover's face. He knew that expression. Blake was up to something.

"I'm planning on throwing a New Year's Eve party here at the office a week today, and I'll be inviting Melissa."

Will stared in shock. *What the hell?* Blake saw his look of consternation and squeezed Will's hand reassuringly before turning his attention back to Justin. "I have a plan, but for it to work, Melissa mustn't have a clue as to what happened today, especially the part about Will." He gazed earnestly at Justin, who nodded.

"You have my promise—not a word. And for what it's worth? I'm sorry about trying to organize your love life." He shivered. "Although I have to say I'm relieved. Fixing you up with Melissa was me doing Bill a favour. I never liked her." He tilted his head. "Not going to tell me what you're up to?" Will liked the sparkle in Justin's eye. He couldn't believe the difference in him. Blake seemed overjoyed to see his father's transformation. What crossed Will's mind was how much time the two men had lost. They had a lot of catching up to do.

Blake chuckled. "No, I'm not telling you—*either* of you." Will widened his eyes. "Not that I don't trust you, babe," he said, leaning forward and giving Will a quick peck on the cheek. "But I have something special planned."

Justin cleared his throat, and Will was tickled to note the blush on his cheeks. Blake's endearment and physical display of affection had caught him by surprise, too. Will liked this new, more confident Blake very much.

"Let's get back to the party, shall we?"

Blake winked at Will. "Sounds good to me." They exited the office and followed the sound of music and laughter into the conference room.

The six people sitting around the table all looked relaxed and happy. They looked up expectantly as Blake, Will and Justin entered the room.

"'Bout time you lot got 'ere." Ed poured out three glasses of wine and handed them over. Blake opened his mouth to protest in some way, but Ed cut him off. "'An don't give me that 'Don't drink 'n' drive' shit. Yer dad's got a driver, so 'e can give ya a lift 'ome, can't 'e?" He beamed at Blake. "C'mon, boss, it's not every day you come out, is it?" He winked at Will. "Not to mention announcin' you've already got a bleedin' boyfriend!" He leered at Will. "You kept that quiet, mate. We didn't 'ave a clue."

"Speak for yourself," Rick added under his breath, winking at Will, who grinned.

Will leaned close and whispered in Rick's ear. "Your secret is safe, cutie. I'll never tell him. Promise." Rick gave him a look of pure gratitude.

Blake stared at his team. "You're really okay with this?"

Peter snorted. "Why would we not be? We already put up with Rick, don't we? And I mean, let's face it—if we can put up with Rick...."

"Hey!" Rick's indignant tone had everyone laughing.

"I think it's really sweet," Lizzie sighed. Beside her, Beth agreed.

Blake's look of incredulity was touching. Will bumped shoulders with him, grinning.

Ed held up his glass. "A toast, folks. To the boss and his fella. A Merry Christmas to the both of ya. Cheers."

The toast echoed around the room, amid the clink of glasses.

"May I make a toast?"

Everyone turned to look at Justin who stood with his glass raised. "To the owner of Trinity Publishing, Blake Davis, who has proved beyond a shadow of a doubt that he can run this company better than I ever could." He faced his son. "Which knowledge I plan to share with the world out there as soon as I can give my statement to the press." The two men shared identical grins. Justin's words were followed by *woots* and shouts from the team. Blake beamed at his team.

"Can I ask something?" Rick's voice rose above the noise. All eyes turned to look at him. Rick's eyes gleamed with mischief. "I for one would like to see the boss kiss Will." There were gasps but Rick snorted. "Oh, don't give me that, you lot. You want to see it as much as I do." Laughter greeted his words. Will saw Blake glance at Justin but his father waved his hand, grinning widely.

"Don't look at me. They're your team—keep 'em happy. It *is* Christmas, after all."

Shaking his head in disbelief, Blake beckoned Will with his finger. "Come here." Will walked slowly up to him and moved in close. Blake murmured under his breath. "I don't believe we're doing this."

Will chuckled. "To quote you from a short while ago—kiss me."

Blake's hands reached around to cup him at the nape and pull his head closer, their mouths meeting in the merest brushing of lips. Will closed his eyes, stifling a moan as Blake grew bolder and deepened the kiss, both men getting into it.

Will had no idea how long they stood there, but at last they parted, Blake's eyes shining as he gazed at Will.

The applause started almost instantly. Beth and Lizzie stared at them, wide-eyed.

"That was so beautiful." Lizzie's voice was choked with emotion. Rick was staring at them with a look so full of longing that Will decided to make it his New Year's resolution to find him a man of his own.

"Love you."

Blake's words cut through his thoughts. He gazed at his lover in wonder. With those words, Blake had just changed their lives. Will could only guess at what else lay in store for them in the future. But as far as Christmas Eve was concerned, Will knew exactly what he wanted to happen.

He wanted to go home and make love to Blake.

CHAPTER THIRTEEN

"You didn't need to do that, you know."

Blake stirred from the cozy world he'd lost himself in and regarded Will as he lay stretched out in his arms on the sofa. "Hmmm? What do you mean?" He was thoroughly content. Dinner had been a joint effort and it had felt so good, just the two of them, laughing and joking as they prepared the meal. Definitely something Blake could get used to. And now that they were lying together on the sofa, Will sprawled on top of Blake, the thought was even more inviting. The fire burned behind the glass, and the lights from the Christmas tree danced over the walls and ceiling as they reflected off the glittering baubles which adorned it.

"You didn't have to tell those officers that we'd been together all night." Will reached up and stroked his cheek with soft fingers. "They'd have worked out I had nothing to do with it once they saw there was no evidence."

Blake pulled his arms tighter around Will. "I wasn't thinking straight. All I could see was them dragging you away in handcuffs, and I couldn't stand it." He kissed the top of Will's head lightly. "I had to say something."

Will twisted in his arms to gaze up at him. "Do you regret it?" He bit at his lower lip.

Blake tugged him until Will's face hovered above his. "Not for a second." Will's pupils dilated and Blake cupped his head to draw him closer, their lips meeting in a gentle kiss.

They parted and Blake stared into Will's eyes. "Love you." The thrill it gave him to finally say the words.

There was that look on Will's face, the one from the photo. "Love you, too." Will kissed him, their lips brushing together sensuously. Will let out a long, drawn-out sigh. "Oh, it's been so good, staying with you every night this last week. Waking up with you." He snuggled against Blake, his body warm and familiar.

Blake loved the little contented noises that slipped from Will as he lay in Blake's arms. "Yeah, I've loved having you here." So much so that it was a wrench each time Will left.

Will kissed the tip of his nose. "Do you know how hard it's going to be to go back to my little flat for Christmas." His plaintive sigh tugged at Blake's heart, which suddenly leaped in his chest as a thought infiltrated his brain and wouldn't leave.

"Then don't go. Stay." Blake's voice shook slightly.

Will stared down at him, his forehead wrinkling. "You want me to stay for Christmas?"

Blake shook his head. "No, I want you to stay for good." His heart hammered as he awaited Will's reaction. Will's eyes grew large and round, his lips parting.

"You mean it?" The words came out as a whisper.

"With all my heart." He gazed up into those warm chocolate eyes that he'd come to love so much. "Move in with me."

Will became so still above him, their eyes locked on each other. Blake felt as though his whole body was tingling with anticipation.

"Yes," breathed Will, and then he kissed him, the kiss starting out slow and sensual, but with a growing sense of urgency.

Blake caught his breath as Will began to slowly unbutton Blake's dark blue shirt, freeing each button with deliberate care, until at last he pulled aside the garment and began to kiss Blake's chest, the kisses unhurried as he licked at his warm skin. Blake whimpered as Will caught his nipple between his teeth and tugged gently. He felt Will's chuckle reverberate against his chest. Will flicked the nipple with his tongue before releasing it.

"Like that?"

"Oh yes. More." Blake needed.

There was that wry chuckle again. "Greedy. Be patient." He flicked at it once more, before kissing Blake's abs, tracing a line over them with his tongue, only to cover his belly with soft kisses.

"You're doing this on purpose, aren't you?" Blake gritted out, his breath catching as Will pulled gently at his waistband, bestowing light kisses just above his groin.

Will shifted further down the sofa, until he was resting between Blake's thighs which spread for him. Will chuckled, his hand slowly caressing Blake's hard-on which was already pushing against his zipper. "My, we *are* eager tonight." His fingers plucked at Blake's belt, tugging it free of the belt loops and tossing it onto the floor, and then returning to unbutton Blake's pants. He caught the zipper in his teeth and pulled it slowly, his gaze fixed on Blake.

Blake couldn't tear his eyes away as Will eased his pants over his hips and then mouthed his dick through the tight black briefs which barely restrained it, already damp with pre-come. "Take them off," he hissed.

Will let out a low moan and sat upright, tugging eagerly at Blake's pants, socks and briefs, dropping them into a pile near the sofa before pulling Blake up to remove his shirt. Blake shivered in anticipation as he began to undress his lover, his fingers trembling as he removed every stitch of clothing, until at last Will was naked before him, his skin warm in the firelight. Blake got up from the sofa and taking Will's hand, led him to the rug where 'Alec' had fucked him three months ago. Both men sank down into the thick pile, stretching out on their sides, head to tail. Blake licked at the heavy, thick cock in front of him, and then took Will into his mouth, sucking him deep, groaning out loud as his dick was engulfed in the hot, wet furnace of Will's mouth. For several long minutes, the only sounds which filled the room were small cries and whimpers as they worshiped each other's cocks, hands sliding over warm flesh to caress each other. Blake licked and sucked at the thick shaft, moaning as Will deepthroated him.

He released Will's cock with a gasp. "You're going to make me come," he panted breathlessly.

Will pulled away from his shaft which glistened with saliva. "Isn't that kind of the idea?" he heaved out, his eyes heavy with lust. Blake turned and pushed Will onto his back, his face inches away.

"I want to be inside you when I come."

Will's pupils dilated even further, until there was barely a trace of brown to be seen. "Oh God, yes."

Blake bent to take his mouth in an urgent kiss, cupping Will's face in his hand.

Will grabbed Blake's hand and pushed it down insistently toward his cock, murmuring into his mouth, needy, urgent sounds that had Blake's dick rock hard. Blake broke the kiss and fed a couple of fingers into Will's mouth, whimpering as Will sucked at them eagerly, getting them wet. He pulled them free of his mouth, only to push one finger slowly into Will's tight channel, Will's staccato sounds of pleasure music to his ears.

"Does that feel good?" Blake whispered close to Will's ear as he pressed deeper into Will, searching for his gland. Will's low cry burst out of him as Blake nudged the small bump inside him. His eyes pleaded with Blake as his hips rocked up from the floor in gentle thrusts. Blake grinned and steadily pushed a second finger into him, Will's mouth opening wide as he arched up from the rug, shaking.

Blake freed his fingers and rolled on top of Will, undulating sensuously against him as they kissed, a collision of lips and tongues. Blake ached to be inside him. He leaned toward the coffee table and pulled open a drawer, scrabbling around inside until his fingers found their prize, a strip of condoms and a tube of lube. He knelt and tore off a foil square, holding it up for Will to see. "Ready for me?"

"Blake, have... have you ever barebacked?"

Will's question stopped him dead. He gazed down at his lover. "Never." But of course now the idea was in his mind. The thought of sliding bare into Will sent his pulse racing and his cock twitching. "Are you asking me to—"

"No," Will hastened to add. "I just wondered if..." His words died away, but Blake's heart gave a jolt as he saw the expression in Will's eyes. Will wanted to, that much was plain.

Blake placed the packet on the rug beside him and pulled Will into an upright position to straddle him, his legs winding around Blake's waist. Blake wrapped his arms around his lover, pulling him close. "How about we both get tested?" he said at last. "And then we'll take it from there." He kissed Will lingeringly on the mouth and pushed up with his hips, loving the feel of his cock rubbing over Will's hole. Will clung on to his shoulders as they kissed, his moans increasing as Blake's movement grew more heated.

"Inside me. Please." Will leaned back, his weight on his arms as he watched Blake cover himself quickly with the latex, and then squeeze lube onto his rigid shaft. Will was shaking with need as Blake lifted him slightly to press the head of his cock against his hole. Will lowered himself into position, letting out a low, heartfelt groan as Blake filled him completely. "Oh fuck, I can feel every inch of you."

Blake clung to him, pushing up slowly with his hips. "Oh God, so deep inside you." They began to move slowly together, quickly establishing a rhythm, Blake pushing up into Will with slow, deliberate thrusts, Will shuddering as Blake grazed his gland, his eyes fixed on Will. "You feel so good, baby." Blake fought the urge to speed up his thrusts. He had a plan. "You need to tell me when you're getting close. Because we're going to make this last as long as we can, all right?"

Oh God. Will had always wanted to indulge in a little edge play.

He clutched at Blake's back as he rode his cock, whimpering as the thick shaft slid up inside him. The way Blake watched him so intently was so sexy, his eyes fixed on Will as he slowly pushed up into him, his body rippling as he concentrated on making Will feel good.

"Oh my God, babe, that feels...." It felt too damn good. "Getting close."

Blake stilled inside him, his hands stroking down his back as they kissed, Will coming back from the edge of the precipice where he'd been teetering only seconds earlier. "That's it, baby, make it last." Blake explored his mouth with a leisurely tongue, Will mewling as warm hands slid around to caress his chest, pulling gently at his nipples. Fuck, Blake was driving him out of his mind.

"Ready for more?"

Will was about to reply in the affirmative, when Blake grabbed hold of him and lowered him onto the rug on his back, Blake's cock still deep inside him. Blake pushed Will's thighs toward his chest and hooked his arms behind his knees to pin him to the floor. Leaning low over Will, Blake proceeded to push into him, each thrust slow and measured, and all the while his eyes never left Will. It was exquisite torture.

Blake's face hovered barely an inch above Will's, his breath warm against Will's cheeks.

"Love being inside you."

Will whimpered.

"Love pushing all the way into you, feeling your arse wrapped tight around my cock." Will cried out as Blake gave a forceful thrust, his balls slapping against Will's cheeks. "Love watching your face when I'm inside you, feeling your body tighten around my cock when you're coming." Will moaned as Blake began to rock into him more quickly. "Like now. Your face is so beautiful when you're about to come."

Will's breathing grew more erratic as Blake powered into him. His body tingled. "Cl-close, Blake!" He reached down to tug at his cock, but Blake brushed it away as his thrusts slowed.

"That's mine. You don't touch."

Will stifled a howl. Fuck, what Blake was doing to him...

Will lost all count of the number of times Blake brought him close to orgasm, so close that it felt as though one more thrust of Blake's cock would send him tumbling over the cliff into ecstatic oblivion. And then he would ease off, leaving Will almost sobbing with both relief and frustration. Yet he knew—when he was finally allowed to come, it was going to be like nothing he'd ever experienced.

Blake pulled out virtually all the way, until only the head of his cock remained inside him. He speared Will with such an intense gaze that it left him reeling. In that one moment Will could almost believe Blake could see every thought in his head. Blake grabbed Will's hands and pinned them above his head by the wrists. He hovered above him, his lips tantalizingly near.

"Ready to come?" Those blue eyes saw him, saw the need in him.

"Yes," Will whispered, "God, yes. Now, please, babe." He was shaking, his whole body balanced on a knife edge of desire.

Blake smiled. "I love you." His mouth took Will's as he thrust powerfully into him, hips snapping forward as he slammed into him repeatedly. Will cried out into his mouth as white light exploded behind his eyes, his cock jetting come onto their bodies as Blake froze, arching his back to howl in ecstasy. Will felt the pulse of Blake's cock deep inside him, felt Blake tremble with the force of his climax, and he just... let... go.

Oh God, it was like... Will felt as if he were floating, as wave upon wave of intense pleasure surged through his body, the euphoria like nothing he'd ever experienced. He was aware of Blake's body covering his, Blake's lips on his mouth, his neck, his chest. And still those hands held him firmly, anchoring him to the floor as his orgasm flowed through him, leaving him trembling in its wake. Blake murmured into his ear, soothing sounds that warmed him, reassured him of his lover's presence, Blake's cock still inside him.

Will lay shaking as aftershocks jolted through him, dissipating gradually until his pulse returned to normal, his breathing less erratic. Blake released Will's wrists and rubbed each one tenderly, before easing himself out of Will, holding the condom in place. For one fleeting moment Will imagined feeling the slow trickle of Blake's come as it leaked out of him after making love. One day.

"Oh my God, Will, that was..." Blake regarded him with a look filled with wonder.

Will reached up and cupped his cheek. "Perfect. That was perfect."

He pulled Blake down into a tender kiss. He could feel Blake's heart beating in time with his as Blake rolled him onto his side and wrapped his arms around him, holding him close, his leg hooking over Will's hip to draw him even closer. They lay on the rug, warmed by the fire as they held each other, the only sounds their even breathing as they kissed and caressed one another, the outside world lost to them for the night.

Blake had always dreaded Christmas. It had been an awkward time growing up, just him and Justin, and in some ways Blake felt as though he had been robbed of the childhood magic of Christmas, something which he could never get back.

Will changed all that in one day.

From waking him up with fresh coffee and croissants, to putting on Christmas carols which filtered quietly through the apartment, to preparing their lunch together... Will had given them both a day filled with magical memories—not to mention some very sensual, intimate ones. Blake was continually amazed by how attuned Will was to him, both in bed and out of it. They could have been made for each other. And didn't *that* thought send heat radiating through him. Blake felt so light, he could have floated.

The day was almost derailed by a phone call. Dinner was over and Blake lay stretched out on the sofa with Will lying in his arms. It was fast becoming his favorite position. The warbling of his phone was an unwelcome intrusion into the peace of the day. Will reached for the phone and passed it to him with a frown. Yeah, he knew how Will felt. Blake's heart sank when he saw Melissa's name on the screen. He knew he'd have to talk to her sooner or later—right now later sounded much better.

"Melissa, what can I do for you?" There was no way he was about to indulge in pleasantries with the bitch. He saw Will's eyes widen as he sat up. Blake pulled himself upright.

Her nasal voice was loud in his ear. "Well, and a Merry Christmas to you, too!"

He sighed heavily. "Merry Christmas." He'd gone over in his head a thousand times what he intended to say to her, but hearing her voice brought back all the pain she'd caused them. "I expected to see you at the office yesterday." Not that he wasn't relieved when she hadn't shown up. It made what he was about to do a lot easier.

"Yeah, well, Daddy took me out for lunch." There was suddenly a hard edge to her voice. "So, have you considered my proposal?"

Blake guffawed. "Proposal? That makes it sound like I have a choice."

She huffed. "Don't get difficult about this. Because I can make life really uncomfortable for you if you do."

Not any more, Blake thought. Okay, now for his plan...

"There's going to be a New Year's Eve party at the office next week. You're invited. I'm going to be making an announcement at that time and I really need you to be there." He winked at Will, who stared back at him, a crease between his eyes. Blake blew him a kiss and smiled reassuringly. "Can you make it?"

The note of glee in her voice was all too evident. "Of course! I might have to go shopping for a new outfit just for the occasion."

Blake fought hard to control his laughter. "That sounds like a good idea. You'll want to look your best." He gazed at the man next to him and all of a sudden he was in no mood to continue the conversation. "Sorry, Melissa, I have to do some online shopping. I'll see you at the party. It'll start at eight. Have a good Christmas." Before she could say another word, he ended the call.

Will took the phone away from him and then regarded him closely. "Care to share any of this with me?"

Blake shook his head. "No. It's going to be a surprise for everyone." His expression softened. "I can promise you one thing, though. You'll like it." He winked. "But I guarantee Melissa won't." He leaned forward and kissed Will softly on the lips. "Now, what say we go back to what we were doing before we were so rudely interrupted?"

Will's face creased into a beautiful smile. Blake liked that answer.

CHAPTER FOURTEEN

"Mr. Parkinson, could I have a word with you and Mr. Davis, please—in private?" Karen spoke in a low voice.

Will stiffened. Karen hadn't said a word to him during the last three days. She'd returned to work on the Tuesday morning, her face looking less bruised, but she had studiously avoided him. He knew Blake had requested an interview with her, but that she'd been less than forthcoming. They were still both clueless as to why she'd accused him. But it saddened him that he'd gone from being 'Will' to 'Mr. Parkinson.'

He glanced around the conference room. The preparations were all but complete. Lizzie, Rick and Beth had decked out the room in balloons, and the food Blake had ordered now weighed down the table. Peter had rigged up a sound system and was busily putting together the music for the party. It was to be a real family affair. Blake had instructed the team to invite their partners and families. He'd even invited Dave. Justin was due to arrive shortly.

Karen was regarding him anxiously, twisting her watch around her wrist. Will glanced at the clock. There was plenty of time before the party was due to start. "Come on, let's step into Blake's office." Karen let out a huge breath and gave him a grateful smile. Will led her to Blake's office. The door was ajar. Blake was going through a set of folders on his desk, tidying things up. He looked up in surprise to see Karen with Will. "Is there something wrong?"

Before Will could say a word, Karen launched into a speech that she'd clearly been preparing. Will struggled to keep up with her, she spoke so fast.

"I had to speak to you both, to apologize for what I did last week. After I spoke with the police, they decided not to press charges, but only because I told them what was really going on. You see, I—"

"Karen, slow down." Blake gestured toward the sofa. "Sit down for a minute, please."

Karen took a breath and then walked to the sofa. She eyed them both warily. Blake sat at the other end of the sofa. Will stood leaning back against Blake's desk, watching her as she fingered her necklace. Will noted for the first time that her style of dress had changed. Gone were the tight blouse and skirt. Karen wore a dark pair of pants and a modest yet elegant blouse.

"Okay, now let's start again." Will loved Blake's calm manner. "Who did this to you?"

Karen stared first at Blake, then at Will, her cheeks gradually becoming more flushed. "My boyfriend, Tom." The words were delivered in a hushed tone.

Will stared incredulously. "Then why on earth would you tell the police that it was me?" He was dismayed to notice fat tears welling in her eyes, spilling out over her cheeks.

"Because he made me say it!" Karen wailed. Will and Blake regarded each other, frowning. "It's all my fault."

Blake got up from the sofa and entered his bathroom, returning with a wad of toilet tissue which he handed to Karen. She blew her nose loudly.

He retook his seat, looking distinctly unhappy. "Karen, you can't blame yourself. He did this to you."

"Yes, but it was because of something I did." She hiccuped. "He came to pick me up one evening after work, and saw me leaving the building with Will. He...he saw me touching Will's arm, and..."

Will recalled the event instantly. Karen had been her usual flirtatious self. "But that was weeks ago." She nodded miserably. Something occurred to him. "Karen, has he ever hit you before?"

She stiffened. For a moment there was silence, and then finally she whispered, "Yes."

Blake groaned. "Then for God's sake, why did you stay with him? Why not leave?"

Karen stifled a sob. "He kept telling me that I was useless as a girlfriend, that no one would ever love me. And then he'd tell me how lucky I was that *he* stayed with me. I heard it so many times this last year, it got so that I believed it."

Will's heart went out to her. He knew it was common for someone in an abusive relationship to put up with such treatment, the lengths they would go to in order to keep someone. But it still didn't answer his question. "So why tell the police it was me?"

She twisted the tissue in her hands. "He kept on at me, asking me if I was seeing you, if I was interested in you. I told him the truth, but he wouldn't believe me. Finally, he just... snapped." She wiped her eyes. "He knew he'd gone too far when he woke up the next morning and saw the state of me."

Karen raised eyes full of misery to stare at Will.

"Tom s-said I was to tell the police that you'd done it, that if I didn't, I-I'd get a l-lot worse." The tears started up once more. "I know it was stupid, but I wasn't thinking clearly. Anyway, once I told the police everything, they arrested Tom and charged him with assault. They got me to fill out a restraining order, so that once he made bail, he couldn't come near me."

"So you *have* left him?" Blake regarded her doubtfully. When she nodded, he let out a relieved sigh. "Well, that's something."

"Karen, for what it's worth, I'd like to offer you an apology." Will knelt in front of her. Karen's eyes widened in surprise. "I'm sorry for the way I behaved that day in the kitchen. I shouldn't have lashed out at you like that."

Karen pressed her lips together. "I was so angry with you. It was humiliating, knowing that I'd been throwing myself at a gay man for all those weeks. And you let me!" Will felt a pang of guilt. Then her lower lip trembled. "But that doesn't excuse what I did." She stared down at the hand he held out to her, and then she took it. He squeezed her hand tight.

"It's over, okay?" Will affirmed, meeting her gaze. He felt a surge of relief as she nodded at last. Impulsively he leaned forward and kissed her cheek. Karen blushed.

"Are you staying for the party, Karen?" Blake wanted to know.

She regarded him, biting at her lip. "I-I wasn't intending to. I thought the team might feel awkward if I were here."

"Rubbish," Blake said briskly. "They're all relieved to see you. Of course you're staying." He winked. "Besides, you don't want to miss *this* party. Trust me."

Will wondered for the umpteenth time that day what Blake had up his sleeve. He rose from his kneeling position to stand once more by the desk.

Karen got to her feet and gave her nose a final blow. "Thank you, Mr. Davis, and you too, Mr. Parkinson."

Blake sighed. "Let's go back to 'Blake' and 'Will', what do you say, Karen?" She considered his words for a second or two and then nodded, smiling weakly. Blake clasped her hand and watched as she exited the office.

"Well, I'm glad that's sorted," he said with a wry smile. "How are things looking out there?"

Will gave a grin. "Looking good. The troops have things well in hand." He took Blake by the hand and pulled him up off the couch, sliding his arms around him. Blake's eyes gleamed.

"And what are you up to?"

Will cupped his chin and kissed him, the kiss slow and sweet. Blake closed his eyes and Will pulled him closer, loving the feel of his body snug against him. When their lips parted, Will stepped back, already regretting the loss of Blake's warmth. "About my Christmas present..."

Blake gazed at him with a wide smile. "Did you like it? There's nothing quite like holding a book with your name on it, I'm reliably informed."

Will's gut clenched. Opening the book that Christmas morning had been a delightful surprise, but he'd had time to think on it since. "Look, I want to talk about this. I—"

There was a knock at the door and Rick poked his head around it. "Boss, your dad's here." He withdrew.

"Great." Blake kissed Will on the tip of his nose. "Let's continue this conversation later, okay?"

"Sure." Will wasn't sure what he was going to say, however. He needed to make some things clear. Blake headed out of the office, Will following him. Justin was standing in the corridor outside the conference room, a wry smile on his face as he observed the feverish preparations. He caught sight of Blake and grinned.

"This looks really good. How many people do you have coming?"

Blake counted off on his fingers. "The team, plus various partners and family members, Dave Thurston, Melissa..." His eyes widened. "Dad, did you invite Bill Richards, like I asked you?"

"I didn't have to. Melissa had already gotten there before me. It seems she's really looking forward to this party for some reason." He winked. "Can't think why." Both men shared a chuckle. "So, are you going to tell me what you have up your sleeve?"

Blake gave him an evil grin. "Nope. You'll just have to wait."

Justin rolled his eyes. "Are you sure you want my son in your life, Will? He can be *very* annoying."

Will grasped Blake's hand and squeezed. "I'm sure." He and Blake exchanged a look, one that made his legs go weak. God, the effect this man had on him...

Noise behind them signalled the arrival of the first guests, and Blake released his hand. "I'll go greet people."

He gave Will a quick peck on the cheek. "Can you get my Dad sorted with something to drink?" Will nodded and Blake gave him a winning smile as he walked off. Will turned to find Justin regarding him with affection.

"I haven't seen much of you two since we last spoke,"

Will held back a snicker. It was hardly surprising. Blake hadn't let Will out of his sight all week. Every minute where they weren't at the office, they'd spent in each other's company. The Sunday after Christmas had been moving day and it had been such a wonderful feeling to finally close Blake's front door behind him and realize he was home. The thought made him smile. Home was where Blake was.

"You really do love him, don't you?"

Will came back into the moment and met Justin's gaze. His reply was heartfelt. "Yes, sir."

Justin put his arm around Will's shoulders and squeezed. "I'm so glad you're in his life, Will. I've never seen Blake so happy."

If Will had his way, Blake would be happy for the rest of their time together. He'd see to it personally.

It was nearing midnight. The party had been going really well. Melissa had turned up fashionably late, her father in tow. Will could only estimate how much she'd spent on her outfit. He scowled. She wasn't doing it to please Blake. She simply wanted to look fabulous when Blake announced their engagement. The scowl faded, to be replaced by a grin. He couldn't wait to see the look on her face.

His thoughts were interrupted by the sudden silence as the music was switched off. Blake motioned for him to come stand nearer. Justin and Bill were deep in conversation, and both looked up to see what was happening. Melissa was hovering near Blake, her eyes gleaming.

Everyone in the room turned to face Blake as he stood at the end of the room.

"Thank you all for coming here tonight. I know some of you put off attending large family gatherings to be here tonight."

"Hey, boss, we should be thanking you!" Rick's outburst had everyone laughing.

Blake grinned. "And some of you might even have been planning to join the crowds on the riverbank to watch the fireworks."

"Yeah, okay, we're 'appy to be 'ere, all right?" Ed's cheerful interjection caused more laughter.

Blake held up his hand for silence. "As I was saying, it was really important to me to have you here tonight. I'm particularly grateful to have my team around me." He held up a glass of champagne. "Guys, you are the best people it has been my pleasure to know. You give 100 percent, every day, and this company wouldn't be where it is without all your hard work." Applause greeted his words. Blake turned to his father. "Dad, thank you for the wonderful press release this last week. To have you praise all the things we've achieved here was one of the best things that's ever happened to me. I hope to make you even more proud of me as Trinity Publishing goes from strength to strength." There were murmurs of approval from his audience.

Blake lowered his glass and gazed at the people around him. Will found the hairs standing up on his arms. He shivered. All his senses told him something was coming.

"Someone said to me recently that New Year's Eve is a very romantic time to announce an engagement." Out of the corner of his eye, Will was aware of Melissa beside him. He gave a brief glance in her direction. Her eyes gleamed with triumph. "That got me thinking. After all, New Year is a time for new beginnings, resolutions, a time to cast off bad habits and take up new ones. So it is with that in mind that I have to share something personal with you all."

Will caught the buzz around the room. All eyes were fixed on Blake, his included.

"I've met someone, someone who means the world to me. We haven't known each other for that long, but when you meet the person you're going to spend the rest of your life with, your heart knows it. Time is immaterial."

Will's chest constricted. What the hell.... His heart raced as Blake pulled a small, black velvet box from his pocket and walked slowly toward him. Will felt his legs tremble. Surely Blake wasn't going to....

"Will Parkinson, I love you. I don't want to spend another minute of my life without you." Will gasped as Blake got down on one knee, holding out the open box, where a simple white gold band inset with diamonds gleamed.

Beside him, there was a sharp intake of breath.

Will ignored it, his attention focused solely on the man kneeling before him, his upturned face glowing with love. "Marry me, Will?"

The murmurs and gasps of the room's occupants faded away as Will gazed into his lover's eyes. His heart pounded in his chest as he reached down to cup Blake's cheek. "Oh God, yes." The smile that spread across Blake's face sent him soaring. Blake got to his feet and after removing the ring from its box, slipped it onto Will's finger, sliding it into position. He moved closer, until Will could feel the heat pouring off him.

"I love you, so much." Blake murmured the words, before cupping the back of Will's head to pull him into a kiss that rendered him breathless. Will was oblivious to everything but the man who held him so closely. He lost himself in the heady kiss, Blake's breath sweet as he sighed into his mouth. From the back of the room the applause started, building until it reverberated off the walls, accompanied by shouts and hollers of support.

"What the *fuck* is going on here?"

Melissa's strident voice cut through the joyous sounds. Blake and Will parted, stepping back. Melissa's face was a mottled shade of purple, her eyes almost bulging from her head as her face contorted. She glared at them.

"This was *not* what we agreed!"

Blake regarded her coolly. "What exactly did we agree, Melissa?" Will was suddenly aware of the horrified glances Bill was giving his daughter.

"You know what I'm talking about! You were supposed to be proposing to *me*!"

Blake laughed, the harsh sound so unlike him. "I'm gay, Melissa. Why would I propose to you?" Her lips narrowed and her eyes became slits. "Oh, that's right, I forgot. I was supposed to marry you and make you rich, and in return you wouldn't tell my father that he had a *fag* for a son." The cold gleam in Blake's eyes made Will shudder. "That *was* the deal, wasn't it?"

Bill Richards glared at his daughter. "What is Blake talking about, Melissa?" Will watched as all the colour slid from Melissa's face. Her mouth opened and closed as she stared at her father.

Justin gave his friend an apologetic look. "I'm sorry you had to hear it like this, Bill. The boys informed me last week about Melissa's little blackmail attempt. Fortunately, events took a different path." Melissa gaped. He walked across to Blake and Will and put his arms around their shoulders. "I'm delighted to hear their news, and I'm sure I speak for everyone here." There were enthusiastic murmurs from all around. Justin levelled a scathing look in Melissa's direction. "Well, *nearly* everyone."

Melissa marched over to Blake and spat in his face. "And that's for making me spend all that money on this outfit. Do you have any *idea* what I paid for this?"

Bill growled. "That's enough."

Blake reached into his wallet and pulled out a wad of banknotes. He flung them in her face. "I wouldn't want you to be out of pocket." He ground out the words as the notes fluttered to the floor. As she bent down to pick them up, Bill grabbed hold of her arm and hauled her upright.

"Leave it. You're acting like a little whore." A look of disgust crawled across his face. Will felt Blake take his hand. He swallowed. His hand firmly around Melissa's upper arm, Bill turned to Justin. "I'm sorry about this, Justin. I'm going to leave now, so you can all get on with enjoying the party. After all, it's nearly midnight." He glared at his daughter who had started to blubber. "Melissa and I are going to have a little talk about her future, and how she's going to cope *without* my money in her bank account." Melissa's eyes were huge as she stared at her father. He gave a brief nod in Blake and Will's direction. "Congratulations to the pair of you, and my sincerest apologies for whatever pain she put you through. I can only imagine how you must have felt." And with that, he marched Melissa from the room, her sobbing becoming more audible. The members of Blake's team watched her departure with cool glances.

Justin clapped his hands together. "Fill your glasses, please, ladies and gentlemen. Midnight fast approaches." Rick and Beth rushed around the room, making sure everyone had a full glass. Peter opened the window and in the distance could be heard the sounds of the crowd counting down to the chimes. Justin held aloft his glass. "As New Year arrives, I'd like to make a toast. To Blake and Will, with many blessings for their future happiness together." His words were echoed around the room as the first chime rang out from Big Ben. "Happy New Year, everyone!"

Amid the sounds of glasses clinking and best wishes being exchanged, Will turned to Blake, his eyes glowing. "Happy New Year."

He kissed him softly, closing his eyes as he savoured the silky touch of Blake's lips against his. When they finally parted, Blake gazed at him, a glint in his eye.

"I for one don't like the idea of a long engagement. I don't know how you feel on the subject, but I don't want to wait. I want our future to start as soon as possible."

Will grinned. "You're going to drive me crazy, aren't you?"

Blake's returning grin was even wider. "You have *no* idea."

Will was sure he'd have fun finding out, though.

EPILOGUE

"I'm home, babe!"

Will leaned back in his chair and stretched. "In here!" Perfect timing. He'd just finished the scene and was feeling mentally drained. He saved the five thousand words he'd written that day and closed the laptop, knowing full well that within half an hour, he'd be back on it, tweaking, adding and deleting until he was happy with it. Will wiped at his damp eyes.

"Heavy scene?" Blake was standing in the doorway to the dining room which now doubled as Will's office, leaning against the doorjamb, his jacket slung casually over his shoulder, tie already off and shirt unbuttoned at his neck. Will felt his cock stiffen at the sight of his gorgeous husband. *Maybe the tweaking can wait for a while.* He held his breath as Blake strolled purposefully to stand behind him, slipping warm hands under his shirt to stroke his chest and tease his nipple into tight little nubs. Blake's lips ghosted down his neck, making Will shiver with anticipation. "Need a little down time?"

Will leaned his head back and waited for the kiss he knew was forthcoming. Blake didn't disappoint him. Will's mouth was taken in a hungry kiss, Blake's tongue demanding entrance, exploring him eagerly, even as he slid his hand lower to rub over the bulge at Will's crotch. Will groaned into his husband's mouth, loving the way Blake could get him from lukewarm to raging hot in minutes. *Minutes? Seconds.*

Blake pulled away, and Will was shocked to hear the whimper that he let escape. Blake chuckled. "Later, okay?"

"Tease," he growled, pushing the heel of his hand against his now rigid cock. He glanced at the wall clock and straightened immediately. "I lost all track of time!"

Blake gave him a knowing smile. "Yeah, that's an occupational hazard for you these days."

Will ignored the gentle barb. He knew once he got into a book, they could drop the bomb and he wouldn't notice. Focus was definitely not a problem. As long as he ignored the call of Facebook, that is. "Have you heard anything yet?" he demanded impatiently.

Blake shook his head. "You?" Same reaction. He pulled out his phone and inspected the battery level. "We should have heard something by now."

Will gave a wry smile. "How long did it take last time? Eighteen hours?"

Blake grimaced. "Oh God, don't remind me. All that waiting was driving me crazy! Anyway, the second is usually quicker." Will arched his brows and Blake gave a shrug. "So they tell me."

Will snickered. "And it's only been"—he consulted his watch—"four hours, thirty-five minutes and fifteen seconds since you called to tell me Lizzie was in labour." He grinned. "Your godson will get here in his own good time." He got up from his chair and kissed Blake lightly on the lips. "I'll make some fresh coffee. Want some?" Blake gave an absentminded nod, his thoughts clearly on Lizzie and Dave.

"Who's got Milly?" Blake asked as he followed him into the kitchen

Will laughed as he reached for the coffee and started preparing the machine. "Not me, thank goodness!" Their three-year-old goddaughter was a bundle of energy who left them both exhausted each time she came to visit. Dave would laugh every time, mocking their lack of stamina. "I think Rick and Angelo have her—God help them." Will met Blake's gaze. "You still sure you want to do this? When Milly stays here, it's like a mini tornado has hit the place."

Blake stilled. "You're not having cold feet, are you?"

Will cursed himself for putting that crease between Blake's eyes. He hastened to reassure his husband, drawing Blake into the circle of his arms. "No, baby, not at all." He kissed Blake tenderly. "And it won't be long now. I'm sure Donna will be ringing us any day now with good news."

The phone warbling into action startled them both. Blake's eyes widened and Will watched his hand shake as he connected the call. "Dave? Is everything okay?" His face erupted into a huge smile. "Oh, that's great news! How's Lizzie?" Will poured two mugs of coffee and placed one in front of Blake, who beamed at him. "How much does he weigh? Wow. Poor Lizzie." He snickered. "Tell her she can hit me when she sees me later tonight. We'll be there for visiting hours, armed with a teddy bear. And does our godson have a name yet?" Blake's lip trembled and Will was disturbed to see tears welling in his eyes. "Oh Dave, that's... that's wonderful." He listened intently for a minute. "Yeah, I'll pass that on. We'll see you later. And Dave? Thank you."

Blake disconnected the call and stared at the screen in silence for a moment.

Will waited impatiently, his heart pounding. At last he couldn't take any more. "Well?"

Blake raised damp eyes to stare at him. "Eight pounds four ounces." Will winced. "Justin William Thurston."

Oh. Will pulled Blake to him in a fierce hug, kissing his hair, his cheeks, before finally taking his mouth in a kiss full of sweetness. He broke away, wiping at his own eyes which were suddenly blurry. "Justin would have got a kick out of that." He sniffed. They'd only lost Justin a mere six months ago, his second heart attack having proved more lethal than the first. At least he and Blake had spent the last five years building a new relationship. And as for Will, losing Justin had been as painful as if he were Will's own father. The two men had grown really close.

Will led Blake into the living room and pushed him insistently to sit on the sofa. Will curled up next to him, sharing his warmth. Blake draped an arm around him, pulling him close.

"The saddest thing?" Blake stared into space. "Dad will never get to see his grandchild." They'd spent the last year finding a surrogate, and

Donna was perfect. Both men had donated sperm at the clinic. It didn't matter to either of them who the baby's biological father would be. It would be *their* child.

Will kissed his cheek. "I'm sure he'll know. I believe that." Blake gave him a watery smile. "And it's great news about Dave and Lizzie." He chuckled. "Who'd have thought it? Inviting Dave to that party all those years ago changed both their lives."

Blake looked at him keenly. "Just how many years ago was that, now?" His eyes twinkled.

Will snickered. "No, I haven't forgotten. The champagne is in the fridge and the deli chicken is in the oven." He cupped Blake's cheek and kissed him on the mouth. "Happy fifth wedding anniversary, Mr. Davis—and of course, Happy 36th Birthday." They spent several minutes doing nothing but kiss, slowly and languidly, both content to enjoy the moment.

Blake broke the kiss to take a drink from his mug. His eyes went to the bookshelves where one shelf had been given over to Will's books. Will saw the direction of his gaze.

"Do you ever regret firing me?" Will bit his lip, waiting for the usual outburst. He didn't have to wait long.

"I didn't fire you!"

Will burst into a peal of laughter. "Oh yes you did. I can still hear every word you said that day. You told me I needed to do something else with my life, and that you'd support me in every way you could while I concentrated on my writing."

Blake grumbled. "Well, could you have carried on working under me?"

Will leered. "Oh, but I love being under you."

Blake smacked his arm. "Be serious."

Will grinned. "Oh, but I was being *very* serious." He waggled his eyebrows and then pouted as Blake hauled himself up off the sofa and walked over to the bookshelf. Will knew without looking exactly what Blake was doing.

Sure enough, Blake turned around with a familiar volume in his hands. Will had to smile. "Be careful with that. It's a very rare item."

It was the copy of his book, Out in the Cold, that Blake had produced for him that first Christmas together. The only copy in existence.

"Do you ever regret not letting me publish it? It could have been huge, you know."

Will shook his head. "It was the right decision, babe. It was far too personal to me. And there was always the chance that someone would recognize me from it. I didn't want people rooting around in my past. Besides, that chapter of my life is over." He glanced over at the row of books which represented the last five years of his life. He gazed up at his husband. "I've never regretted leaving Trinity. Working on my writing has been so fulfilling, not to mention lucrative." His latest gay thriller had been out for over two months now, and it hadn't budged from the top five at Amazon. And of course the success of the books had finally helped to pay off the last of his student loans. Their conversation was still so clear in his head, like it was yesterday. He vividly recalled his reaction when Blake had offered to support him.

"I did...what I did because I wanted to pay off the loans. I appreciate the fact that you're offering to help, but you have to understand. If I take money from you for this? It seems like I'm still whoring myself to pay for them." Blake opened his mouth to speak, but Will raised a hand. "I didn't say it was logical. It's how I feel. Please say you understand."

The corners of Blake's mouth turned upward. "Yes, I understand. What I was going to say was I think that's an incredible attitude to have and shows strength of character."

"Enough introspection, Mr. Davis." Blake grinned suddenly. He'd been so happy when Will had asked to take his name after the wedding. Will had no inclination to keep the name Parkinson. It only served as a reminder of the family who had cast him aside. Justin had been more of a father to him in their five years as a family than he'd ever dreamed possible.

Blake came over to the sofa and extended a hand to him. Will took it, puzzled. Blake pulled him to his feet. Blake wrapped his arms around Will and held him close, murmuring into his ear, his husky voice doing delicious things to Will's cock.

"We have a few hours until it's time to go to the hospital. Dinner only needs heating up, and the champagne can wait until we get home." Blake tugged gently at Will's earlobe with his teeth. Will shivered. "And let's not forget, today is also another anniversary. Six years ago tonight, babe." He gestured toward the rug. "The new bottle of lube is in the coffee table drawer." He winked.

Will grinned. "I'll fetch the leather shackles."

The End

If you enjoyed this book, then please take a look at the rest of the series. And if you can leave a review, that would be wonderful. Reviews help keep books visible.

And if you keep scrolling, you'll find an extract from the next book in the series, Personal Changes

Personal Changes

"Morning, Boss." Rick greeted Blake with his usual cheerful grin. He helped himself to a coffee in the small kitchen that served their floor. "I didn't expect to see you in here today."

Blake tilted his head as he poured out two mugs of coffee. "And why would I be taking the day off?" He regarded Rick with amusement. "I don't recall the second of January being a national holiday, last time I looked."

Rick smirked. "Yeah, but after New Year's Eve I figured you and Will might have wanted a little time to yourselves. I mean, you did get engaged, right?" Rick waggled his eyebrows. "I'm sure you were both up late, seeing the New Year in." Another suggestive leer. "Among other things."

Blake paused mid-action and turned to face him. "Is this what I'm going to get every morning? The third degree about my private life?" The barest hint of a smile told Rick his boss hadn't really taken offense, but Rick knew Blake. It was time to back off.

His voice softened. "Sorry, Blake. And for the record, I think it's wonderful. You two make a beautiful couple." That much was true. Blake with his black hair and amazing blue eyes, and Will with dark, brown hair and those eyes the color of milk chocolate—they made a striking pair.

And I'm trying desperately to forget the fact that I've been lusting after you for six years.

The previous week's Christmas party had been quite the night for revelations. When Rick had got over the shock that not only was his straight boss definitely *not* straight, he was also in love with his PA, Rick's first thought had been one of regret. When Blake had taken him on as part of his team, Rick had fallen in lust with him within a very short space of time. Of course, he'd never gone there—Rick had been burned enough times by making advances to straight guys to know that making a move on his dishy new boss would probably have had him out the door on his arse. It was bad enough that Will knew his secret.

"Aw, that's sweet." Will came into the kitchen and grinned at Rick, before taking the mug Blake handed him. "Thanks, babe."

Blake shot Will a warning glance. Will's grin faltered, until Blake patted his arm, smiled at them both and then exited the kitchen with his coffee mug. Will watched him go, an unreadable expression on his face.

"And what was that look all about?" Rick sensed a little tension in the air.

Will huffed. "We had a talk this morning, that's all, about my future here. Oh, and how we were going to play things from now on."

"Let me guess. Act professional, no being all lovey-dovey."

Will nodded glumly.

Rick chuckled. "I suppose that means you've seen the last of any shenanigans in his office."

Will groaned. "Oh God, don't remind me. Besides, he has a point. I mean, look what happened that last time he and I..."

He didn't have to finish. Blake's would-be fiancée Melissa hadn't exactly caught them having sex in Blake's office, but had seen enough to make their lives miserable. At least she was out of the picture now. *And good riddance.*

Something Will had said finally registered. "Back up a minute. What do you mean, talking about your future here? You're not leaving, are you, Will?" Rick bit his lip. Will had only been with them for three months but in that time he'd become a good friend.

Will slurped his coffee and gave a low moan of appreciation. Blake made really good coffee. He warmed his hands on the mug. "Let's just say he's not happy about me continuing as his PA now we're engaged." Will scowled. "The jury is still out, however, on whether I quit. I don't want to—I still have my student loans to pay off, after all—but he says it's something we need to consider seriously."

Rick patted Will's arm. "Now don't you two fall out about this." Not that he could see much coming between the two men. Watching them together at the New Year's Eve party a couple of nights ago had been just beautiful. Rick had to admit, the two men really fitted each other. Never mind that it had only been three months since Will had strolled into Trinity Publishing and into Blake's life. *When you know, you know*, he reasoned with himself. *And the heart knows what it wants.*

Will smiled. "Don't worry about us. We'll sort it out, trust me." He levelled an intense stare at Rick. "But what about you? Made any New Year's resolutions?" He tilted his head. "And you know I'm talking about your love life here." His expression softened. "We need to find you a guy, Rick. I'm going to make it my mission this year." He gave a decisive nod.

Rick snorted. "Good luck with that."

Will's brow furrowed. "What do you mean?"

Rick let out a sigh and sipped his coffee. "I haven't been as lucky as you and Blake in that department. I seem to have lousy taste in men."

Will eyed him keenly. "Have you been looking? And if so, *where* have you been looking?"

Rick thought for a moment and then walked over to the door. He pushed it shut and leaned back against it. Will regarded him curiously.

"Look," Rick began, lowering his voice, "the longest relationship I've had lasted three months. Men don't seem to want to stick around me. So now I take what I can get."

"What does that mean?" Will's voice was suddenly as low as Rick's.

Rick expelled his breath. "It means I go to a lot of clubs and I have a lot of casual sex, okay?" His eyes met Will's. "That comment I made a while ago about being in toilet stalls with guys? I wasn't kidding." He lowered his gaze.

"Aw, Rick, I didn't know that's what you were doing." Will stepped closer and gave Rick a brief but firm hug. Rick closed his eyes. It had been a while since anyone had hugged him. When he opened them again, Will moved back and gave him a stern look. "I don't have to ask if you're being safe, do I?"

Rick's chest tightened. Will was a good friend. "No, you don't. I may be a slut, but I'm not stupid."

The crease between Will's eyes deepened. "I don't like it when you talk about yourself like that."

Rick shrugged. "I'm just being honest, that's all. I like sex, I'm not ashamed to admit that. And yes, every Friday and Saturday, you'll probably find me in a club, chatting up some bloke before going home with him or taking him back to mine." He met Will's gaze. "But if I found someone who wanted to do the whole monogamous route, someone who wanted us to be serious about each other?" He smiled. "I'd be off the club scene so fast, you'd get whiplash watching me leave." His heart felt heavy. "Right now, there doesn't seem to be anyone out there who wants me like that, so until then, I'll carry on being careful and always leaving my flat with a supply of condoms."

Will looked sad as Rick opened the door to go to his office, ready to start work, coffee mug still in his hand.

"I'm going to keep checking on you, all right?" Will said earnestly.

Rick blew him a kiss. "You're a sweet guy, Will, and Blake's a very lucky man." He paused in the doorway. "Thanks, mate. I'm glad we're friends."

"Always." Will's tone was serious. "And you can come talk to me anytime, you know that?" Rick nodded.

"Okay. Then get to work, lazybones." His eyes sparkled with good humour.

Rick tugged his hair in a subservient gesture. "Yes, sir. Right away, sir." He winked. "Got to keep in with the boss's boyfriend, after all." He ducked as Will picked up a tea towel and threw it at him, missing him by inches. Rick laughed and walked along the corridor to his office.

Time to get some work done. He had a host of advance review copies to send out to review sites, not to mention setting up time for authors to meet their readers on Trinity's Facebook page. He could get some of it done before Blake's morning team meeting. *No rest for the wicked.* And the way he was feeling right now? When Friday night got here, he intended being very wicked indeed.

Find your copy here![1]

About the author

K.C. Wells lives on an island off the south coast of the UK, surrounded by natural beauty. She writes about men who love men, and can't even contemplate a life that doesn't include writing.

The rainbow rose tattoo on her back with the words 'Love is Love' and 'Love Wins' is her way of hoisting a flag. She plans to be writing about men in love - be it sweet and slow, hot or kinky - for a long while to come.

If you want to follow her exploits, you can sign up for her monthly newsletter: http://eepurl.com/cNKHlT

You can stalk – er, find – her in the following places:

Email: k.c.wells@btinternet.com

Facebook: **www.facebook.com/KCWellsWorld**[1]

KC's men In Love (my readers group): **http://bit.ly/2hXL6wJ**

Blog: kcwellsworld.blogspot.co.uk

Twitter: @K_C_Wells

Website: www.kcwellsworld.com

Instagram: **www.instagram.com/k.c.wells**[2]

BookBub: **https://www.bookbub.com/authors/k-c-wells**

---

1.   http://www.facebook.com/KCWellsWorld

2.   http://www.instagram.com/k.c.wells

Also by K.C. Wells

Learning to Love
    Michael & Sean
    Evan & Daniel
    Josh & Chris
    Final Exam
Sensual Bonds
    A Bond of Three
    A Bond of Truth
Merrychurch Mysteries
    Truth Will Out
    Roots of Evil
    A Novel Murder
Love, Unexpected
    Debt
    Burden
Dreamspun Desires
    The Senator's Secret
    Out of the Shadows
    My Fair Brady
    Under the Covers
Lions & Tigers & Bears
    A Growl, a Roar, and a Purr[1]
    A Snarl, a Splash, and a Shock[2]
    Love Lessons Learned
    First[3]
    Waiting for You
    Step by Step[4]

---

1.   https://books2read.com/u/3JR8lB
2.   https://books2read.com/SnarlSplashShock
3.   https://books2read.com/u/3LwlZD

Bromantically Yours
BFF[5]
<u>Collars & Cuffs</u>
An Unlocked Heart
Trusting Thomas
Someone to Keep Me (K.C. Wells & Parker Williams)
A Dance with Domination
Damian's Discipline (K.C. Wells & Parker Williams)
Make Me Soar
Dom of Ages (K.C. Wells & Parker Williams)
Endings and Beginnings (K.C. Wells & Parker Williams)

<u>Secrets – with Parker Williams</u>
Before You Break
An Unlocked Mind
Threepeat
On the Same Page
<u>Personal</u>
Making it Personal
Personal Changes[6]
More than Personal
Personal Secrets
Strictly Personal
Personal Challenges
Personal – The complete series[7]
Confetti, Cake & Confessions
(FREE)[8]

---

4.   https://books2read.com/u/bzdA1n

5.   https://books2read.com/u/3JnzKE

6.   https://books2read.com/u/3RYVDR

7.   https://books2read.com/u/mYx6kG

Christmas
Connections
Saving Jason
A Christmas Promise
The Law of Miracles
My Christmas Spirit
A Guy for Christmas
Dear Santa[9]
Santa's Secrets[10]
Island Tales
Waiting for a Prince
September's Tide
Submitting to the Darkness
Island Tales Vol 1 (Books #1 & #2)
Lightning Tales
Teach Me
Trust Me
See Me
Love Me
A Material World
Lace
Satin
Silk
Denim
Southern Boys
Truth & Betrayal
Pride & Protection
Desire & Denial
The Southern Boys Trilogy[11]

8.   https://www.prolificworks.com/book/33626

9.   https://books2read.com/u/bMw8E8

10.   https://books2read.com/SantasSecrets

<u>Maine Men</u>
Finn's Fantasy[12]
Ben's Boss[13]
Seb's Summer[14]
Dylan's Dilemma[15]
Shaun's Salvation[16]
Aaron's Awakening[17]
Levi's Love[18]
Maine Men – the Complete Series[19]
<u>Salvation</u>
Wrangled[20]
<u>Second Sight</u>
In His Sights[21]
In Plain Sight[22]
<u>CrossBow Protection</u>
Broken Warrior[23]
<u>Standalones</u>
Kel's Keeper[24]

11.   https://books2read.com/u/m2l0NG

12.   https://books2read.com/FinnsFantasy

13.   https://books2read.com/u/md77JW

14.   https://books2read.com/u/m2RjJR

15.   https://books2read.com/u/bQV6pv

16.   https://books2read.com/ShaunsSalvation

17.   https://books2read.com/u/mvWWvz

18.   https://books2read.com/LevisLove

19.   https://books2read.com/u/bMz8J7

20.   https://books2read.com/Wrangled

21.   https://ooks2read.com/u/4NoWOW

22.   https://books2read.com/u/3GGadK

23.   https://books2read.com/u/3R5DwB

24.   https://books2read.com/u/b5vjV6

Here For You
Sexting The Boss
Gay on a Train
Sunshine & Shadows
Double or Nothing
Back from the Edge
Switching it up
Out for You[25] (FREE)
State of Mind[26] (FREE)
No More Waiting[27] (FREE)
Watch and Learn[28]
My Best Friend's Brother[29]
Princely Submission[30]
Bears in the Woods[31]
Holy Hell – with Parker Williams[32]
Teasing Tim[33]
Str8 B8[34]
Anthologies
Fifty Gays of Shade
Winning Will's Heart
Come, Play
Watch and Learn

---

25.   https://www.prolificworks.com/book/62550

26.   https://www.prolificworks.com/book/74720

27.   https://www.prolificworks.com/book/82301

28.   https://books2read.com/u/boEK9Z

29.   https://books2read.com/MyBestFriendsBrother

30.   https://books2read.com/PrincelySubmission

31.   https://books2read.com/u/3LRVLX

32.   https://books2read.com/HolyHell

33.   https://books2read.com/u/bOJRAW

34.   https://books2read.com/u/4X0dj6

<u>Writing as Tantalus</u>
Damon & Pete: Playing with Fire[35]

---

www.ingramcontent.com/pod-product-compliance
Lightning Source LLC
Chambersburg PA
CBHW022153260626
47155CB00017B/1857